Jeannie & the Gentle Giants

OTHER BOOKS BY
LUANNE ARMSTRONG

Maggie and Shine
(Hodgepog Books, 1999)

The Colour of Water
(Caitlin Press, 1998)

Arly and Spike
(Hodgepog Press, 1997)

The Woman in the Garden
(Peachtree Press, 1996)

Bordering
(Ragweed Press, 1995)

Annie (Polestar Press, 1995)
Also published in Germany by Beltz & Gelberg.

Castle Mountain
(Polestar, 1981)

Jeannie &
the Gentle Giants

Luanne Armstrong

RONSDALE PRESS

RONSDALE PRESS
3350 West 21st Avenue
Vancouver, B.C., Canada
V6S 1G7

Set in Minion: 12 pt on 16
Typesetting: Julie Cochrane
Printing: Hignell Printing, Winnipeg, Manitoba
Cover Art: Robin LeDrew, "Jeannie meets Sebastien," gouache
    on paper, 17-1/2" x 12"
Cover Design: Julie Cochrane

Ronsdale Press wishes to thank the Canada Council for the Arts, the Government of Canada through the Book Publishing Industry Development Program (BPIDP), and the Province of British Columbia through the British Columbia Arts Council for their support of its publishing program.

National Library of Canada Cataloguing in Publication Data
Armstrong, Luanne, 1949–
    Jeannie & the gentle giants

    ISBN 0-921870-91-4

    I. Title.
PS8551.R7638J42 2002   jC813'.54   C2001-911044-8
PZ7.A757Je 2002

*This book is dedicated to
the late Art Twomey, a man gentle
in his ways — a man of the
mountains who loved animals,
wilderness, laughter
and friends.*

ACKNOWLEDGEMENTS

With thanks for all their help to Anthony Arnold and his beautiful horses, Hannah Rose, Mary Sutherland, Robin LeDrew, Dr. Carolyn DeMarco, Joanna and Alan Wilson, Mary Woodbury, Mary Billy, K. Linda Kivi, Margaret Elliott, and of course, my wonderful children and grandchildren. I wouldn't be anywhere without all of you. Thanks.

Chapter One

Jeannie held her breath.

"Look sharp now, young one," Arnold roared. The huge tree swayed, crackled all along its length, and thundered to the earth. The ground shuddered under her feet where Jeannie stood holding the reins of two giant workhorses that stood beside her, blowing jets of steam into the cold damp air.

"Okay," Arnold said, coming back from where the tree stretched its bristling length across the ground. "Get your axe, little one. Time to get to work. Get those limbs off."

Jeannie got a small axe and began awkwardly chopping the smaller limbs off the top of the tree trunk the way

Arnold had shown her, while Arnold took the big limbs off
with his chain saw. Then Jeannie began dragging the limbs
to the fire Arnold had lit that morning. As she threw them
on the fire, they hissed and crackled and sent up plumes of
white smoke. As the needles on the branches caught fire,
the flames leapt roaring into the air and the heat reached
crisp fingers to toast Jeannie's already red face. Her hands
were black and sticky with pitch.

Arnold backed the team of workhorses up to the end of
the log and wrapped a chain around it. "Hup," he said.
"Hup, Seb. Git up there, Sal." The powerful horses lowered
their heads, dug in their huge feet, and the log slid easily
behind them, down the trail towards the pile of logs already
waiting for a truck to come and take them to the sawmill.
Arnold came back up the trail with the team.

"C'mon, kid," Arnold roared. "Enough hay-down. Let's
have some lunch." He fetched two piles of hay from the
truck parked beside the logs and put them down for the
horses. He slipped off their bridles and put on halters so
they could eat. Then he brought their own lunches and set
two round pieces of log by the fire to serve as seats.

Arnold's partner, Katie, came from where she had been
marking the trees they would cut later in the afternoon.

Jeannie was starving. Her foster mom had packed her a
big lunch, a thermos full of soup, two cheese sandwiches, a
carton of juice, and a chocolate bar. She sat down beside the
fire as far from Katie and Arnold as she could get. She kept
her head down, eating her lunch.

For a while there was only the sound of munching from the clearing in the middle of the huge green cedar and hemlock trees.

"Well," said Arnold, leaning back. "That feels a whole lot better, hey kid?"

Jeannie tried to ignore him. He was so weird. She had a name. You would think he could learn to use it. So far, he had called her everything but her name. He had called her punkin, kid, little one, young one. Anything but her real name. And he talked funny. He hardly said anything that made sense. Well, she didn't have to be nice to him or to anyone else for that matter. None of this had been her idea, not the foster home, not coming to a new community, away from everything she knew, and certainly not coming to work outside in this damp, miserable, cold forest.

Arnold laughed softly. He was a big man with a bushy black beard, bright blue eyes and teeth that flashed white in the middle of a deeply tanned face. He wore heavy wool pants, held up by striped suspenders that went over a green and black checked shirt.

"Boy, oh boy," he went on, "I sure do love to stop for lunch. I guess that's just about my favourite part of the day. I do believe Sally and Seb feel the same way. What about you, Katie-did, don't you think lunch is the best part of the day? Now I could sure use a pot of tea, boiled up over the fire to finish it off. What do you two think?"

Jeannie glanced at him from under her long brown bangs, which hung down into her eyes. Then she looked at

Katie. Katie wore her brown hair in two long braids. She had brown eyes and her face was tanned too. She wore the same kind of clothes as Arnold. Katie was nodding. "Yep, a cup of tea would go down pretty good right now."

"Well, Miss Jeannie-with-the-light-brown-hair, want to fetch us a pot of water from the creek?" Arnold asked.

"Not really," she said in a tight, tiny voice. After all, she had done everything he had asked all morning. She had worked harder than she had ever worked at anything else in her whole life even when she was scared to death that a tree would fall on her head or the horses would step on her with their huge feet.

So he could make his own tea. She didn't even drink tea. She was only eleven years old. Her mom always told her she was too young for tea or coffee, that juice or plain water was good enough for her.

"Well, gosh darn it all," Arnold roared with laughter. "Guess I'll have to do it myself." Jeannie couldn't see what was so funny. After all, she had just been really rude. And he had laughed.

"Is he always like that?" Jeannie whispered to Katie, after Arnold had gone whistling off to the creek to fetch water for tea.

"What do you mean, honey?" said Katie.

"Does he always laugh at everything?"

"He sure does, sugar. He just thinks the world's a strange and wonderful place. He can find something to laugh at in most things."

"Well, I wish he wouldn't laugh at me," she said. "He's really weird."

She got up and went over to the horses. They had finished their hay and were nosing around on the ground for more. Jeannie found some stray bits they had missed and held them out flat on her hands, as Arnold had shown her. They nosed at her hands with their huge lips. She scratched their chests and necks. They towered over her. Her head barely came to the top of their legs. Their heads were almost as long as she was tall. She leaned against their powerful warm bodies, keeping her face away from Katie.

When she had first seen the giant horses driving into her foster parents' yard, she had been astonished. She had never seen such a thing. Since that terrible afternoon when her mom had gone off in the ambulance, nothing had seemed normal to Jeannie. Things had moved so fast. First her mom disappeared behind the grey walls of the hospital, then after a few days in some horrible place called a group home, the social worker came by to tell her she was being placed in a foster home, out in the country, far from the town where she had lived her whole life.

"I don't want to go away," Jeannie tried to tell the social worker, whose name was Robin. "I want to stay here with my mom." She was terrified that if she left the town, she would never see her mother again.

"Honey, your mother isn't well enough to see you right now," Robin said. She sat on the worn pink bedspread beside Jeannie in the tiny cubicle that Jeannie had been told was her room. Robin's voice was soft and sugary. She was trying to be really nice but Jeannie didn't care.

"As soon as she is feeling better, your foster parents will arrange a visit. It's a very nice home, and it's the only place we can find for you right now. As soon as a place opens up in town, we'll move you back here."

Jeannie hung her head and stared at the floor. She didn't want to listen to Robin. She didn't want to be told what to do.

All Jeannie wanted was her mother back and for their life together to continue. Life with her mother hadn't been easy. They moved a lot from place to place. Jeannie's mom had a lot of jobs but none of them seemed to last. Sometimes her mother spent days wrapped in a blanket in a chair, but Jeannie had learned to wait for her to come out of these bad times. When her mom was happy, she was really happy, full of plans and ideas, crazy fun things they could do together. Sometimes they'd stay up all night, finishing some project, and Jeannie wouldn't bother going to school the next day. School was boring anyway. Her mom, Judy, said she could learn more at home reading books. Sometimes they spent the whole day together at the library.

Judy had been a dancer when she was younger. She had long straight black hair, a slim body, thin brown hands. Jeannie hoped that when she grew up she could be as beautiful as her mother. Right now, Jeannie thought herself pretty ugly. She was tall and thin, with long straight brown hair. Her face was thin too, with freckles and green eyes. Her feet and hands were too big for her skinny body. But that would all change when she grew up, her mom said.

"Don't worry about that, Jeannie," she laughed. "You are my shining angel. You are beautiful inside. That's what counts."

But her mom worried about everything else so much. Sometimes, at night, Jeannie could hear her mom crying into her pillow, trying not to make too much noise.

When her mom was unhappy, Jeannie could always think of something to cheer her up. She'd make her mom soup from a can and make sure she ate. She'd turn the TV on to her mom's favourite program. She'd draw her mom pictures or tell her things that had happened at school.

But lately her mom had been really unhappy. She told Jeannie the neighbours were bad people, they were always looking in the windows. Once she told Jeannie she thought there were UFOs, hiding outside their building, spying on them.

"That's not true, Mom," Jeannie would say firmly. "Our neighbours are okay. There aren't any UFOs. I looked."

"My head hurts, Jeannie," her mom moaned. "I can't stand this pain."

Jeannie would get her mom some aspirin and make her a cup of mint tea with lots of honey. That always made her mom feel better. Before Jeannie went to school each morning, she'd make sure her mom had a cup of tea and some aspirin beside her bed. She'd make sure the TV remote was where her mom could find it. Some days, when Jeannie came home, her mother was still lying in bed, watching the TV with her eyes half closed.

But then one day something had happened which Jeannie still didn't understand. When she came home from school, there were police cars and an ambulance parked in front of her building. She ran the whole last block. The building door was propped open. She ran up the flight of stairs to her apartment. A policeman was there with a woman who said she was a social worker.

"My name is Robin Wilson," the woman said. "Your mom's had an accident. I'm here to make sure you're okay and to take you where people will take good care of you. Do you have a grandma or anyone you can stay with?"

"I want to see my mom," Jeannie said frantically. "I have to see her. Where is she?"

"She's gone to the hospital," Robin said. "Jeannie, try to understand. Your mom isn't feeling well. She needs some help."

"I can help her! I look after her. She's fine when I'm here. I shouldn't have gone to school today. I shouldn't have left her alone. It's my fault." Jeannie was yelling now. She didn't care how loud she was. She had to try and make them understand. She was the one who looked after her mom. She was the one who always made sure her mom was okay. She had to see her.

"I'm afraid that's not possible right now," Robin said. Her voice was gentle. "If you don't have a grandma or an aunt or someone, you'll have to come with me and we'll find you a place to stay for the night."

Jeannie knew she didn't have any relatives. As far back as she could remember, it had just been her and her mom. Her mom had told her once that her family didn't want to see her. Robin wouldn't listen to Jeannie's continued insistence that she had to see her mom. Instead, she took Jeannie's hand and tried to pull her out of the room.

"I'm sorry, you'll have to come with me. Your mom will be fine. You'll be able to see her in a little while."

Jeannie hung onto the door frame. She turned her face to the wall. Her whole body was shaking. Her throat was on fire but she didn't want this woman to see her cry.

"Jeannie, I know this is really hard. But you can't stay here by yourself and you don't have anywhere to go. I'll take you someplace where people will look after you. I'll check on your mom for you and make sure she's okay."

After a while, Jeannie let go of the door frame. Robin packed a few clothes in a plastic bag and then Jeannie let herself be dragged to the car. She didn't know what else to do. Robin drove to a big white house. There were several kids sitting outside on the lawn when they drove up but no one smiled or said hello. She followed Robin inside, where some more people she didn't know and didn't want to know showed her to a room, gave her some pajamas, and showed her where the bathroom was. Everybody smiled too much. She wouldn't look at them. Finally they left her alone. Later they brought her some food but Jeannie wouldn't touch it. She sat on the edge of the bed. Later, she curled in the middle of it, still dressed. She kept waking up. She tried to sneak out of the room in the middle of the night but the door was locked.

Life hadn't made much sense since that moment.

After a few days at the group home, Robin had announced to Jeannie that they'd found her a foster family, some nice people who lived out in the country. She was sure Jeannie would like them, she said. They were really nice people. Jeannie would have her own room. She could go back to school.

Her new foster parents lived in the mountains to the northeast of Kelowna, the interior town where Jeannie had grown up. Robin drove Jeannie there. They came up a long driveway to a small white house sitting at the top of the hill under some big trees. There were lots of pink and yellow flowers growing around the edges of a bright green lawn.

Jeannie hid behind Robin as they came through the front door.

"This is Susan, Jeannie," Robin said. "She's going to be your new foster mom." Robin had already told Jeannie the details on the way up, about the woman, Susan, who worked in a grocery store, and Tom, who worked part of the time as a carpenter. The rest of the time, he made clay pots in a studio just outside their house. Robin explained to Jeannie that Susan and Tom didn't have any children of their own so they decided that helping foster children might be a good idea. Jeannie was their first foster child.

Jeannie didn't care about anything they said. She kept her head down so her bangs fell over her eyes. She didn't want to be a foster child and she had already decided she didn't have to bother being nice to people she didn't even want to know. She just wanted her mom back and for everything to go back to the way it had been.

Robin and Susan escorted Jeannie up to her new room and put her backpack with her things in it on the bed.

"Take your time settling in," Robin said. "I'll be back to check on you in a few days. Try not to worry. I'm sure everything will be fine."

"There's some cookies and lemonade downstairs," Susan said. She smiled anxiously at Jeannie. Then she looked at Robin to see if what she had said was okay.

That night, at dinner, Jeannie ate with her head down. She gulped her food, paid no attention to her manners, pushed back her chair and went up the stairs to her room. She didn't unpack, just fell asleep curled up in the middle of the bed in her old clothes.

The next day, after breakfast, Susan walked her down the road to the school bus. Jeannie kept her head down on the bus. No one talked to her all day except her teacher. After school, Jeannie hid in her room until supper, gulped her supper again, and scuttled back up the stairs to her room.

She lay awake until she heard Tom and Susan go into their own room. When the house was quiet, she grabbed her pack, slipped out the door, crept down the stairs, eased open the front door, and trudged down the driveway.

She wasn't even sure what direction to take to Kelowna or what to do when she got there. She walked and walked through the dark night. Tom and Susan's house was up a long country road. Only a few cars went by, and Jeannie hid from them. Weird noises came from the ditches beside the road. A giant bird swooped across the road in front of her. Jeannie's heart leapt. She stopped moving. Finally, she realized it was probably an owl and walked on. She wondered if owls attacked people.

The night was full of fear. Jeannie thought of her mom seeing UFOs. What would she do if a UFO landed on the road in front of her? She'd probably die of fright.

Mom, Jeannie thought, terrified. Mom, come and find me. But no one came.

By the time the dark was turning to grey dawn, she couldn't walk anymore. Her legs were rubber. Her feet were on fire. She curled up on a patch of dusty grass under some brush and a policeman woke her up two hours later by bending over her, shaking her shoulder and saying roughly, "Better come with me, young lady."

The policemen who brought her back home warned her not to try running away again. Susan cried and asked

Jeannie if there was anything they could do to make her feel better. Tom hovered over both of them, not saying much.

Jeannie didn't answer. She didn't eat anything, just went up to her new room and sat on the bed.

The room was beautiful. There was a red rug on the floor, blue curtains at the window, a new quilted red and blue bedspread on the bed. There was even a teddy bear sitting on the pillow with a red heart on his chest. Jeannie went and sat in the corner, far away from the comfortable warm bed. There were some comics in the bookshelf. She read those.

That night, Arnold and Katie came driving up in an old wagon pulled by two giant grey horses.

"Come down here, Jeannie," Susan called. "There's someone I want you to meet." Jeannie came down slowly, scuffling her feet, and made her way into the warm kitchen. She kept her head down. She didn't want to meet any new people.

Tom and Susan's house was heated by a big, black wood stove. The kitchen was painted in white and yellow, with yellow checked curtains and a big round wooden table in the middle. The four adults were seated at the table drinking tea.

"Have a cookie, honey," Susan said. "These are our friends, Arnold and Katie. They own those big horses outside. Arnold thought you might like to see them. Do you like horses, sweetheart?"

"I don't know," Jeannie said. She had only seen horses from far away. Policemen rode horses. Policemen had helped take her mom away. She stood by the door, then started to turn away and go back to her room.

But Arnold ignored her turning away. He simply took her hand and led her outside, Jeannie still dragging her feet. When they came close to the horses, she stopped, terrified. She had never imagined that any animal could be so big. She had to bend her head back and look up just to see the top of their heads.

"Here," Arnold said. He took some green cubes out of his pockets. "These things are kind of like horse candy. They love 'em. Just put them flat on your hand, like this."

Reluctantly, Jeannie reached out her hand. A huge grey head bent down to her and soft lips closed over the cube. "Now go close so he can smell you. Blow in his nose and then he'll always know who you are. Horses never forget anything. This boy's name is Sebastien. He is very gentle. He would never do anything to hurt you." Jeannie forced herself to go closer. The giant head bent down again. She felt warm steamy breath in her hair. She smelled the sweet pungent smell of hair and sweat and horse and leather. Gently, reluctantly, she blew her own breath into the giant fluttering nostrils. A large round brown eye looked down at her.

Once, long ago, she and her mom had boarded the Greyhound bus to go to Vancouver. They had gone to the aquarium to see the whales. She felt the way now she had felt at the aquarium. The killer whale had come close to the glass and looked at her. For a moment, everything, the aquarium, the city, the noise, the people, had all disappeared and there had just been her and the whale.

Now she felt the same way. For the moment there was just her and this giant grey creature named Sebastien. From far away, she could hear Arnold's voice.

"Now scratch him on his chest and neck. He loves that."

She rubbed at the grey hair, and felt Sebastien lean towards her. The giant whiskery rubber lips nibbled at her jacket. He let out a deep sigh. A giant pink tongue reached out for her hand. She snatched it back.

"Ah, he likes you, girl," Arnold said gently. "Now come and meet Sally." Jeannie went through the same procedure with Sally, who was a little smaller than Sebastien, but just as gentle.

"Well, it's a bit chilly to stand around out here. We'll come over one day soon when it's warmer and take you for a ride."

Jeannie realized she was shivering as they went back into the warm kitchen. She wondered about the horses. Didn't they get cold, standing out there in the dark? She wanted to get warm blankets and run out and cover them over.

"Aren't they cold too?" she whispered to Arnold.

"Huh? Oh, they've got warm thick horsehair coats." Arnold laughed in his loud booming voice. "They'll shed them in the spring when the weather gets warm."

Jeannie slipped back upstairs to her room. From there, she could look out the window to the horses standing below. Over and over, she remembered that moment when Sebastien's round brown eye had looked into hers.

When she came downstairs the next morning, Susan said, "Do you want to go to school this morning?"

Jeannie looked at her suspiciously. She had to go to school, didn't she? She knew she was going to catch it for running away, but she didn't care. Next time, she was going to be smarter. She was going to figure out when the Greyhound bus ran to Kelowna, and she was going to get on that bus and go find her mother. Nothing was going to stop her, next time.

"No," she muttered finally. "I hate that school. The kids are dumb."

Susan came and sat down at the table, opposite Jeannie. "I know this is really hard for you," she said gently. "I know you miss your mom."

Jeannie said nothing. She just stared down at her bowl of cereal from under her bangs. She knew if she looked at Susan, she might start to cry. She hated crying. It didn't do any good. If she started crying around her mom, her mom would cry too. Jeannie had learned to laugh and pretend to be strong so her mom would cheer up.

"Tom and I thought it might be good for you to have a break from school for a couple of days. I think you need a little more time to settle in. I took today off, but the problem is, Tom and I have to work tomorrow, and we can't leave you on your own."

"I just want to see my mom," Jeannie said in a tiny voice.

Susan sighed. "Jeannie, I already phoned the hospital this morning. Your mom still isn't feeling very well. She's not ready to see you. Arnold and Katie have invited you to spend the day with them. They are logging with their team just a little way from here. It will be a new experience for you. Arnold says you and the horses really hit it off."

Jeannie banged her spoon into the bowl of cereal, smashing the flakes into smaller and smaller pieces. Susan went on, "Today, I thought we could get you a haircut, and then later we could make some cookies."

"Don't want a hair cut," Jeannie mumbled.

"Okay," Susan said. "What would you like to do?"

"Nothing," Jeannie said. "I don't want to do nothing."

She spent most of that day, sitting in her room on the bed, only coming down when Susan called her for lunch. She read all the comics and started in on the books that were in the bookcase. There were a lot of them, old books: *Black Beauty, Lassie-Come-Home, The Yearling, Old Yeller.* She read far into the night.

But the next morning Arnold came to pick her up in his old green truck, which rattled as it came up the gravel driveway. Susan insisted she eat oatmeal for breakfast, then she made her wear a warm coat, hat and gloves. Jeannie didn't know what to expect.

When she got in the truck, she almost laughed. She had never seen such a mess. The floor of the truck was covered with hay, tools, pieces of rope, weird looking bits of leather.

"Hey, hey, Jeannie my girl, we're gonna have a wild day today," he boomed. Jeannie curled in the corner, as far from Arnold as she could get. When they reached the patch of woods where Arnold and Katie were working, Arnold gave her an axe and showed her how to cut the branches off the trees. He lit a fire and had her drag the branches over and throw them on it. Then he made her hold the horses when he was falling a tree. She was kept very busy. This wasn't her idea of a day off at all. Her new gloves were smeared with pitch and ash. Her hair tangled in her eyes. When it was time for lunch, she was ready to fall down with tiredness.

Arnold came back with a pot of water and balanced it on two logs over the fire. He glanced at Jeannie. "Do you drink tea, girl?" he asked. "Or would you like some nice clean mountain water? Best thing in the world that, mountain water."

"I've got some juice," Jeannie muttered.

"Well, that's fine," he said, "but the poor horses are standing there with nothing at all while we're drinking tea and juice and lying by the fire like royalty. Do you feel like taking that red plastic bucket out of the truck and getting them a drink?"

Jeannie nodded. She didn't mind doing things for the horses, and besides, it got her away from Arnold. She went down the trail to the truck and then along another path to the creek. It was dark and spooky under the trees. She had never been in the woods by herself before. Even though Arnold and Katie weren't very far away, it felt like the trees had closed in behind her like a wall. She filled the bucket from the creek, which was trickling its way over green mossy rocks and shiny tree roots. The water sounded like voices talking. On the way back, the bucket banged and splashed against her leg. Sebastien put his big head down and drank almost the whole bucket in a few giant gulps, slurping the water through his teeth. Sally nosed the bucket impatiently.

Jeannie trudged back down the trail for another bucket. Her arms hurt and her shoulder was sore. She wondered what her mom would think if she could see Jeannie now. Her mother seemed so far away. She wondered what her mom would say about Arnold.

"That's great," Arnold said, when she came back and let Sally empty the second bucket. "That's just fine. That's all they need for now. Too much water isn't a good idea when they're working. Now, m'dear, if you feel like making one last trip to the truck, there's some apples and carrots there which they'd love. They want some dessert too, eh, the poor big babies."

"Babies?" thought Jeannie scornfully. "What a silly thing to call them." Except there was something babyish about their big quivering pinkish lips, covered with whiskers, their soft eyes and gentle noses. She got the carrots and apples and fed them from her hands. She was getting more used to the horses now. She wasn't so frightened that they might step on her with their giant feet, or knock her over with their huge bodies.

"Okay," Arnold said. "Guess we can't be lazy forever. Have to earn a living somehow." He went to the horses, slipped on their bridles, and organized the long slippery reins, which he called lines, over their backs. "We're going up the hill a piece, Jeannie my lamb. How'd you like to ride up and save your poor little legs, eh?"

Jeannie stared at him. Ride? Up there? Arnold laughed. Without waiting for an answer, he grabbed her waist and swung her up on Sebastien's back. She almost screamed but then she clamped her mouth shut. She didn't want to show Arnold she was afraid.

"Now that's the place of kings and queens," he said, "and the knights of old. These are the horses they rode to fight dragons. Imagine that. Hang on tight to the hames there," and he put her hands on two knobs sticking up from the thick leather collar that went around Sebastien's neck.

Jeannie clung with both hands. Her legs felt like they were sticking straight out. It was like trying to ride an elephant. When Sebastien started to walk, he rolled from side to side.

"Pretend it's a rocking chair," Arnold shouted. He was behind the horses, following them up the trail. "Just relax."

Of all the dumb advice. Relax? When she was so high in the air that tree branches were brushing her head and if she fell off she'd probably be crushed to death or break her neck. Relax?

"Watch your head," Arnold shouted, from behind her. Jeannie ducked to keep the tree branches from brushing her off Seb's back. She hung on as tight as she could while the horses climbed a trail that seemed to go straight up the mountain.

At the top, Arnold said "Ho," and both horses stopped. "Down you get," he said. "How was that, eh? Did you feel on top of the world? Now you stay here with Seb and Sal while I go knock us down a few trees."

After he left, she stood with the horses. The sun came out and lit up the treetops below her. A warm breeze came and played with her hair. Sebastien nibbled at her jacket and tried to bite off a button. She pushed his head away and he sighed and blew warm horsey breath in her ear. Then he leaned his giant head on her shoulder. It weighed a ton but she liked it. For a moment, she didn't even feel lonely.

From far away, she could hear Arnold's chain saw roaring. With all her heart, she wished that when she went home that night, that she could run in and tell her mom about her adventures, about the giant horses the knights used to ride.

Most of all she wanted to tell how, as she was riding Seb, she had felt, just for a moment, as if she really were a queen, riding on top of the world with all of Seb's gentle strength and power beneath her. It was a brand new feeling, one she wanted to experience again. She wondered if she would ever have the chance.

Chapter Two

Jeannie stared at the money before stuffing it in her pocket. Arnold had paid her for a day's work. He had boomed praise at Susan when he brought her home.

"That little filly's a heck of a worker," he said. "She can come hang out in the woods with me any time. Sure is good with the horses. Hey, little one, want to come work with me again sometime?"

Jeannie nodded and gave him a shy smile before running up to her room to count her money. He was weird but he was kind of nice as well.

Twenty dollars. She had never had that much money of her own. The next day, when Susan called her for school, Jeannie ran eagerly down the stairs. She smiled shyly at

Susan as she ate her Cheerios and drank some apple juice.

"My, you seem happier today," Susan said. "I guess some time away from school did you some good. I fixed you a really good lunch. I hope you like it."

Susan was looking anxiously at Jeannie. Susan always had a little frown of anxiety on her face. She was tall and thin with brown hair tied back in a pony tail. She always wore skirts or dresses with plain brown shoes. She didn't seem very sure of anything. Jeannie had noticed that, whenever Susan did anything, she seemed to worry about it. When Tom was around, she was always asking him what he thought.

"Thanks," Jeannie said. There was an awkward pause. She hadn't figured out what to call Susan yet. Calling her Susan didn't seem right. Most adults had titles, like her teacher, Mrs. Walker.

"Bye," Jeannie said, and went outside to catch the bus. She was excited. Today, if she was careful, she'd be able to leave the school at noon and sneak down to the bus station. Twenty dollars might even be enough for her to catch the bus back to town. She'd have to find out. When she made it to the town, she'd go to the hospital to find her mom. She would make them let her stay there. Her mom needed her. That's what the doctors and everybody didn't understand. Her mom always said Jeannie was the only one who made her feel happier. With Jeannie there, her mom would get better.

As she got onto the school bus, she looked for an empty

seat but there wasn't one. "Come sit here, Jeannie," chorused two girls in the front row. She knew they were called Shannon and Shirley. Shannon patted the seat beside her. Jeannie also knew they lived fairly close to Tom and Susan's house. They were in her grade and both had long blond hair in braids. They wore blue jeans and bright red sweaters. They looked almost the same, except Shirley's face was rounder and she had more freckles. Jeannie didn't want to sit with them but she didn't know what to say without being rude.

The two boys in front of them turned and stared.

"Hey, Jeannie weenie, heard you got in trouble," one of the boys said.

"Yeah," said the other. "I heard you're gonna get kicked out of school for running away. Wow, cool."

"Oh, shut up, you morons," said Shannon. "Jeannie's new here. Don't tease her. She's our neighbour."

Jeannie sat silently beside them the rest of the way to school while the boys and Shannon and Shirley teased each other and exchanged insults over the back of the seat. She didn't want to make friends with anybody. She wanted to leave and find her mom.

She daydreamed her way through school all morning, thinking that soon she and her mom would be together. When lunch hour came, she snuck away from the school. She thought she knew where the bus station was but it was much farther than she thought.

The grey-haired lady behind the counter stared suspiciously at her. "You can't buy a bus fare without permission from your parents," she said. "Next time, have them come with you."

Jeannie returned to class late and Mrs. Walker made her go to the principal's office.

"I'm sorry," Jeannie said. "I went to the store to get some lunch and I got lost coming back." The principal looked at her suspiciously but she seemed to believe Jeannie's story about getting lost.

"If this happens again, I'll have to phone your foster home," she said. "Now go back to class."

That afternoon, Jeannie tried to pay attention in class. It was hard, because Arnold had asked if she could come to work with him again soon and she kept seeing the big horses in her imagination. In art class, she tried to draw a horse, but it didn't look the way she wanted, so she crumpled her drawing and threw it away.

On the way home on the big yellow school bus, Shannon and Shirley made sure Jeannie sat with them again. Shannon had some gum and gave Jeannie a piece.

Shirley said, "I asked you to sit with us because I saw you in your yard the other day. You just live down the road from us. Would you like to come over after school sometime? You could ask your . . . mom . . . or whoever. Or you could come over this weekend."

"Susan is my foster mother," said Jeannie. "She's not my real mom."

"Oh," they said together. "Where's your real mom?"

"She's in the hospital. She's only going to be there a little while. Then I'm going back."

Shannon and Shirley together looked curious. "What's wrong with her?" asked Shannon.

"She's okay," Jeannie muttered. "She just needs some rest."

"Okay, well ask Susan if you can come over. We could watch videos, or make popcorn, or play outside. We've got a tree fort."

Jeannie didn't quite know what to say. She had never had friends who lived close by. She didn't know what a tree fort was.

"Sure," she said cautiously. "But I don't know if she'll let me."

"Tom and Susan know our parents," said Shannon. "They won't mind, as long as they know where you are. Luke and Jason can come too."

Luke and Jason were sitting just in front of them. They turned around. Luke had bright blue eyes and yellow hair. Jason was dark and smaller than Luke.

"Yeah, last weekend was cool," said Jason excitedly. "We played Warrior Princess in the tree fort. I made a bow and arrow for this weekend. My dad helped me."

"I've got a sword," said Luke.

"We could fix up the tree fort some more too," said Shannon. "Our mom said if we wanted she'd make us a picnic lunch and we could eat outside."

"That sounds great," said Jason. "I could bring some hot dogs and we could cook them over a fire."

"We've got lots to do," said Shirley. "We'll have a great time. Jeannie can help with the tree fort. Do you know anything about building, Jeannie?"

"No," said Jeannie shyly, "but I had a job a couple of days ago. I helped someone named Arnold with his horses."

"You helped Arnold?" they all chorused. "Wow, you're lucky."

"Those big horses are scary," said Shirley.

"Weren't you afraid they'd step on you?" asked Shannon.

"Did you go riding?" asked Luke.

"How did you know what to do?" said Jason curiously. "What could a kid like you do?"

"I rode the horses," said Jeannie shyly. "And I held on to them and gave them their food and stuff. Arnold said they liked me."

"Could you take us to visit the horses, Jeannie?" Shirley asked. "Maybe Arnold would let us go for a ride?"

"I don't know," she said. "I guess I could ask."

"Wow," Shannon said, "Arnold's cool. My parents really like him. He knows all about horses."

It was time for Jeannie's stop. As she got off the bus, her new friends all waved.

"See you tomorrow," they yelled.

When Jeannie came in the house, Susan was waiting with a plate of cookies and an anxious smile.

"How was school?" she asked.

"It was okay, I guess," Jeannie said. Susan looked surprised.

"That's great, just great," she said, too enthusiastically. "Jeannie, I had an idea today. I think you could use some new school clothes. We could drive up to Kamloops, all three of us, on Saturday, and go shopping. Would you like that?"

"Some girls asked me to come over this weekend," Jeannie said cautiously. "Is that okay?"

"I guess so," said Susan. "Do I know these girls?"

"They said you knew them. Their names are Shannon and Shirley."

"Oh, yes, the O'Donnell girls. Their parents are friends of ours. Sure, that would be fine, honey. You could go over on Sunday, and Saturday we'll go shopping."

"Okay," said Jeannie. She slipped out of her chair, her hands full of cookies. "Can I go to my room now?'

"Why don't you go outside and find Tom? There's some new kittens down at the workshop. He could show them to you."

"Oh, okay," said Jeannie. This was turning out to be the most amazing day. First, a whole batch of new friends. Now, a batch of new kittens. She skipped outside in the spring sun. Then she stopped. She realized she hadn't thought about her mom since getting on the school bus after school. What if she started to forget her own mother? That would be terrible. She stopped skipping. Here she had been having fun while her mom was locked away in a horrible hospital somewhere. Her feet dragged as she went slowly towards the barn to visit the new kittens. She had to figure out another plan to run away as soon as she could.

There were five fuzzy, tiny kittens in the box beside their purring mother. Jeannie dropped to her knees beside the box. The kittens still had their eyes closed. Some of the kittens were grey, one was grey and orange, and one was covered with black and white patches.

"Which one would you like?" Tom asked, coming to kneel beside her. "You can have one and we'll find good homes for the others."

Shyly, Jeannie pointed to the black and white one. She had never had a pet. Her mom said they moved too often and an apartment was no place for a pet. She picked up the tiny kitten and held it to her face.

"Then it's all yours," Tom said. "You'll have to give it a name. When it's ready to leave its mom, it can sleep with you in your room. Would you like that?" The kitten stuck out its tiny pink tongue and yawned.

Jeannie looked at Tom and nodded shyly. He smiled down at her. "That's great," he said, "just great. Now let's go eat. I'm starved."

Chapter Three

On Sunday evening Jeannie lay curled up in a ball on her bed. She traced the patterns in the patchwork quilt over and over again with her finger. Susan had told Jeannie she had made the quilt herself. She said it was called a log cabin pattern. It was all bright reds and blues and greens mixed up together.

"That's how I feel," Jeannie thought, "all mixed up." Everything was too good. Everyone was so nice. They were all being so nice to her. Susan had taken her shopping on Saturday and bought her new running shoes, new jeans, two bright new sweatshirts, new pajamas, and a new jacket. Jeannie had never owned brand new clothes before. She and her mom got their clothes at the Sally Ann or at Value

Village. After she got home, she had gone over to Shannon and Shirley's wearing her new clothes and they had all played outside until Shannon and Shirley's mom called them in for lemonade and cookies. Jeannie was so tired that night, she went to sleep without even thinking of her mom. Instead, she was thinking of Shannon and Shirley's little sister, Caitlin. Everyone took turns looking after her. No one ever seemed to get mad at her, even when she acted like a little brat, and threw a tantrum because she couldn't climb up in the tree house by herself. Instead, they all climbed down again so they could help Caitlin up into the tree house. It took all three of them shoving and pushing to get her up and then it was just as much trouble to get her down again.

Jeannie couldn't imagine what it was like to be Caitlin, to have a big family, a mom and dad who seemed to love all their kids, land to play on, lots to eat, lots of friends. Caitlin was spoiled, Jeannie thought. She was a spoiled little brat. Maybe next time she could persuade Shannon and Shirley to leave Caitlin at home.

Another thing that had amazed Jeannie was when she realized that Shannon and Shirley were twins. What was it like never to be alone, always to have someone around who was just like you? At first, it was hard to tell them apart. Sometimes, they talked so fast they ended each other's sentences. It was like talking to one person in two bodies.

But after she came to know them better, she noticed that

Shannon was a little heavier than Shirley. She was always talking about food. Shannon was also the bossy one. She was always organizing everyone.

Jeannie flopped over on the bed. She felt lonesome and left out. Everyone else had lots of people. She had always just had her mom. Now she didn't even have her mom, just all these strangers who all knew each other and were too nice.

Jeannie jumped out of bed, brushed her teeth and put on her new pajamas. She looked out the window at the black night sky. She tried to think of her mom, miles away in some kind of big hospital. She wondered if her mom was lonely, if she missed Jeannie as much as Jeannie missed her. Jeannie wondered if her mom knew that Jeannie was thinking about her and missing her. She wondered if her mom would ever get better and they could make a home together again.

Her heart squeezed into a tight little round ball in her chest. Her throat hurt so much from not crying that she could barely breathe. She thought of the little black and white kitten sleeping curled next to its mother. She slipped into her shoes and threw her coat over her shoulders.

Gently she eased open her bedroom door and crept down the stairs. Susan and Tom were watching TV in the living room. Jeannie opened the front door just wide enough to slip through, then she trotted down the sloping gravel drive to the workshop.

The kittens were in a box under the workbench. Jeannie crouched down and lifted the tiny kitten. She put it under her chin and stroked it gently. It curled up in the hollow of her throat and went to sleep. Jeannie leaned against the workbench. She looked out across the lawn.

"Mom," she thought. She wanted to run across the lawn, down the road, run and run until she found her mom. Instead, she sat still, petting the kitten.

Something moved at the edge of the lawn. She blinked, tried to see more clearly across the dim stretch of grass. Maybe she hadn't seen anything. No, there. A brown shape padded into the open, held up its head, sniffing the air. Then it put its head down to the ground, began to trot across the grass towards the shed. Jeannie held her breath. She could see it more clearly now. It was a dog with long brown hair. There was a bowl of dry cat food sitting just outside the door of the shed. The dog went straight to the cat food and ate it in what seemed like one gulp. Then it stuck its head inside the shed.

"Hi, dog," Jeannie said. But the dog leapt backwards, turned and fled across the lawn and into the trees. Jeannie sat on for a while, hoping it would come back, but the cold seeped into her bare feet. Stiffly, she got to her feet, crept back into the house, and up the stairs to bed.

The rest of the week passed uneventfully. Jeannie did her schoolwork, tried to study and pay attention in school, ate supper with Susan and Tom, watched television after she'd done her homework, and then went to bed early. She kept an eye out for the dog. She knew it was still around because she kept putting out extra cat food and it kept disappearing. She stole some scraps from the kitchen and left them at the edge of the lawn. She didn't say much to Susan and Tom and they didn't ask her many questions. She had given up the idea of running away but only temporarily, until she could think of a new plan.

Friday morning at breakfast, Susan said, "Arnold called last night, after you went to bed. He asked if you wanted to come help out tomorrow. He's not going logging. He just wants some help around the farm."

"I guess so," Jeannie said cautiously. Then she remembered her promise. "Maybe Shannon and Shirley could come over later and see the horses."

"Oh, you'll have to ask Arnold about that," said Susan doubtfully.

The next morning Arnold came to get her in his battered old truck. She had forgotten how interesting his messy old truck smelled, hay and leather and horses and grease and gasoline all mixed up together.

When they got to his house, Arnold said, "C'mon punkin boots, I got something to show you." He led her down towards the corral and barn. His big grey dog, Jocko, went with them. "Thought you'd like to meet everyone," he said. There were Sebastien and Sally, lifting their giant grey heads over the corral bars to greet her. Several other horses were busily eating hay from feeders attached to the corral fence.

"C'mere," said Arnold, opening the barn door. Inside the barn were several box stalls. In the far corner, a giant brown mare was standing eating hay. Jeannie peered over the bars of the corral at her. Suddenly a small brown head appeared around the edge of her huge bum.

"Oh, a baby," Jeannie breathed with delight. Arnold opened the gate so they could go in. The mare turned her head to look at them, but the baby came up, sniffing eagerly at their hands for treats and tossing his head. Jeannie scratched his soft fuzzy coat and blew gently in his nose. When she stopped scratching his neck, he grabbed her hand in his teeth.

"Ouch," she said, snatching her hand back.

"Oh, sorry," Arnold said, "I should have warned you. Baby horses can be real brats. They haven't learned their manners yet. Don't let him get away with it. If he tries to bite you again, push his head away and give him a light smack on his shoulder. Say no and he'll gradually get the message."

The colt rubbed against her and she scratched and rubbed him again. He was so soft.

Then Arnold introduced her to the rest of the horses. There was Bess, an old black mare who Arnold said would have a baby in the next few weeks, River, a big brown chestnut gelding, Stony, an Appaloosa riding horse, and Billy, who was a Welsh pony. There were two fat grey tabby cats that also lived in the barn. Jeannie petted them while they curled around her legs, purring.

Arnold buckled halters on Sebastien and Sally and led them outside. Then he got their heavy harness from the barn. Jeannie tried anxiously to help while Arnold patiently showed her various buckles and straps. The horses stood still, occasionally stamping their feet at flies. Finally, the harness was on and Arnold backed the team up to a big green wagon and hitched them up. He lifted Jeannie up onto the seat and then climbed up himself. Jocko jumped into the back of the wagon and sat there as if the whole thing were his idea.

"We're going to practise for the big fall horse show," he said. "The team has to be able to turn quickly, to work together, stay in step and under control. You just watch and learn." For the next hour, Jeannie hung on to the seat while Arnold put the horses through their paces. By the end of the hour, black ribbons of sweat were running down their legs. Sweaty foam had collected under the straps of the harness.

"Okay," Arnold said. "Your turn." He put the warm leather reins in her hands. He showed her how to hold them, and then how to pull and tug to guide the big horses around the ring.

"Hiyup," Arnold said, and the big horses started off at a walk. Jeannie could feel the motion of their heads through the reins.

"Pull to the right," Arnold said. It was so amazing to feel the horses respond to her hesitant tugs.

"Keep the reins tight, but not too tight," Arnold said. "It's kind of like holding baby birds in your hands. You don't want them to fly away, but you don't want to crush them either. Okay, now pull back and say, ho!" Jeannie did and the big horses obediently stopped.

"Okay," Arnold said. "That's enough for one day. We'll turn these guys out and let them roll. That will dry them off and get them covered with so much mud it'll take me days to clean them again."

Jeannie helped Arnold take off the heavy harness. She led Sebastien while he led Sally to the pasture gate. The two big horses trotted away. Then each of them carefully lowered themselves to the ground and rolled and rolled, scratching their itchy sweaty backs on the rough ground. Jeannie, Arnold and Jocko went to the house where Katie had a big pot of macaroni and cheese, blueberry muffins, and apple juice ready for lunch.

After lunch, Arnold showed Jeannie how to clean the leather harness. Then they washed down the wagon with a hose, and Arnold took Jeannie home. On the way home, he said, "I'm gonna need some help getting ready for the big fall show. And I need someone there to help me drive. Think you would like to give it a try?"

"I don't know," Jeannie said hesitantly. "I don't know much about horses."

"Well," he said, "they like you and you like them. That's a good place to start. And that's what life is about, livin' and learnin'. And you got a knack for learning, I can tell. I like the way you handle yourself. When that baby took a chunk out of your hand today, you didn't even yell ouch, just stayed calm. I was mighty impressed, I tell you."

Jeannie stared at him. Then she felt a sudden stab of guilt. She had forgotten all about inviting Shannon and Shirley over to see the horses.

"I got another idea," said Arnold. "I seen you playing with them rascally O'Donnell twins. Now I got three horses standing around in my corral eating their heads off who need some exercise. Do you think you and your friends would be interested in going riding now and again?"

When Jeannie came in the door at Tom and Susan's, she was feeling so happy she stood still and let Susan give her a big hug. Then Tom hugged her too.

"Hey," Tom teased. "You smell pretty interesting . . . let me see, horse, hay, manure, sweat. I guess you had a busy day too." His hands and face were covered in clay dust.

"I got a video for this evening," Susan said, smiling, "I thought we could have our supper in front of the TV. How about you run have a shower, sweetie, and then we'll watch the movie together. And Tom, just look at you, getting my clean kitchen all dusty. Everybody into the shower. Dinner's in half an hour."

Jeannie ran up the stairs, flung her sweaty horsy clothes in the laundry basket, and then had a long hot shower. She dressed in her warm new pajamas, and came back downstairs. Susan had trays with hamburgers, chips, and root beer for each of them. They watched "The Black Stallion", then Susan and Tom hugged Jeannie again before she went off to bed. She didn't want them to hug her but she stood still while they did. Her mom was the only person who had ever hugged her.

Susan gently brushed Jeannie's hair off her forehead. "I'm so glad you had a good time today," she said. "You know Tom and I love having you here. It's good to see you smile."

Jeannie ran up the stairs to bed. Tomorrow, she could take Shannon and Shirley to visit the horses. Arnold had said she could have a riding lesson, then they could help him pick out a name for the new baby. And from now on, Jeannie had a regular date to go on weekends and help Arnold work the big horses to get ready for the horse show.

When she closed her eyes, she could see all kinds of horses, large and small, black, brown, white, grey, and red, running free, tossing their heads, their manes and tails flying in the wind.

"Mom," Jeannie whispered into the darkness. "I miss you so much. I wish you could see me. I wish you could be here." She got out of bed and went to the window. Somewhere out there was the brown dog, lost and hungry. She wished she could help him. Maybe it was time to talk to Susan about it. She might be able to think of some way to help.

Chapter Four

"Okay, now hold on tight." Arnold began leading Billy around the big corral. Jeannie held onto the reins the way Arnold had shown her. She tried to keep her legs and back straight. But being on Billy's back was a lot different than she had imagined. His back seemed to go up and down as well as roll from side to side. He kept tossing his head and trying to dance away from Arnold's restraining hand. Jeannie was tired and sweating in the hot sun. And mad. Plus her shirt was stained with green goo. So far, learning to ride hadn't been any fun at all.

Arnold had made her do everything herself. First, she had to catch Billy and put the halter on. Then she had to lead him to the hitching rail, brush him all over, clean his feet, and wash his face. Then Arnold put on the saddle and bridle.

"Okay," he said cheerfully, stripping them off again. "Now do it yourself."

The saddle was almost too heavy for her to lift. Billy wouldn't let her put the bit in his mouth but then Arnold showed her how to slide her thumb into the side of his mouth so he would open it. Billy's mouth was slimy with green foam which he rubbed all over her clean shirt almost knocking her over in the process. He kept jumping around. Jeannie was terrified that he'd knock her down and then walk all over her.

"Hasn't been ridden in a while," Arnold said cheerfully. "Kind of full of himself, is our Billy-O." He smacked the horse on its bum which, as far Jeannie could see, only made him jump around more.

When she finally had the horse saddled and bridled, Arnold made her lead him to the corral. Then he showed her how to get on and off and made her do it three times. Then he put her legs and hands in particularly awkward positions, stepped back and nodded encouragingly.

"Looks great," he said, "now just try and keep that position." Oh sure.

Finally, they were going to do some riding and Arnold wouldn't even let her ride by herself.

If it was this complicated and this much work, maybe she should forget it, try something easier, like knitting.

"Just try to relax," Arnold said. He was laughing again. He was always laughing. What was so darn funny?

"Okay, I'm gonna let go now," he warned. "You're going to be on your own. Are you sure you're ready. Get those legs on his sides now."

Jeannie only nodded tightly.

Arnold let go of the reins and Billy immediately headed for the side of the corral, where there was nice juicy green grass.

"Pull on the reins, kick your legs, sit up straight," Arnold was yelling all kinds of dumb things. Jeannie could hardly hear him. She was pulling on the reins and kicking with all her might. The stupid horse didn't even care. Finally, she got him stopped, turned around and headed in the other direction. He promptly broke into a trot, heading for the gate. Jeannie bumped around in the saddle, terrified of falling off. When they got to the gate, Billy stopped abruptly and Jeannie slid off over his head and right onto her bum.

Arnold came running up, looking worried. He peered at her to see if she was okay, then said briskly, "Up you get. If you let him get away with that kind of nonsense, you'll never be able to handle him."

Jeannie's face turned red. She had done her best. It wasn't her fault if the stupid horse wouldn't listen.

But she climbed back up in the saddle, tried to arrange her legs in the stirrups the way Arnold had shown her.

Patiently, he rearranged her legs and hands so that she

felt like a silly puppet who couldn't do anything right.

"Okay, I'm going to just walk beside you," he said, "until you get the knack of it." With Arnold there, Billy behaved himself and Jeannie let herself relax a little. "Pretend you're in a rocking chair, just relax and let yourself rock." As they walked slowly around the ring, it did start to feel a tiny bit like a rocking chair. One that was very high off the ground.

All too soon, Arnold said, "Okay, that's enough for one day. You'll be stiff tomorrow. Now slide off, lead him down to the hitching rail, take off the saddle and bridle and hang them up, then you can turn him loose. I'll meet you up at the house."

He disappeared, leaving Jeannie alone with Billy. Jeannie slid off and Billy started rubbing his head on her shirt again.

"Stop that," she yelled, and smacked him hard on his neck. He jumped back, looking scared. Jeannie immediately felt guilty. She hadn't meant to hit him so hard.

"C'mon," she said crossly, yanking on the reins to lead him out of the corral. When he tried to eat some grass she said, "Stop it," in a very loud voice and he did. When she finally got to the hitching rail, it took her quite a while to remember how to undo everything so she could take it off.

Then she realized in horror that she hadn't tied Billy up. He was loose without a halter. She grabbed the halter and a handful of horse cookies and ran after him. As soon as he saw the treats, he turned around and she got the halter on and safely buckled up. Finally, she turned him loose in the pasture, made sure the gate was shut properly and then trudged up the long sloping drive to the house. Her legs ached.

Arnold and Katie's house was made of logs with big windows in front. There was a deck with flowers in boxes around the edge. A stream ran down the mountain behind the house. She could see the pasture, the horses, the corral, and the far distant highway from the deck.

"Come have some lemonade," Katie called. She and Arnold were sitting out on the deck.

Jeannie slumped into a chair. "Riding is hard," she complained.

"It sure is," Katie agreed, "but just at first."

"Billy wouldn't do anything I told him."

"Oh, he's just a brat," Arnold said. "As soon as he figures out he can't push you around, he'll smarten up."

Jeannie sighed. Earlier, she had watched Shannon and Shirley ride while she sat on the fence. They didn't seem to have any trouble controlling their horses. Maybe she was just a loser, maybe riding was something she shouldn't even try.

"You did great for your first time," Katie said encouragingly. "It's always confusing at first. There's so much to remember. But after a while, it all starts to make sense."

Until now, Jeannie had thought Katie was an honest person. But this didn't seem honest. She hadn't done well and nothing had made sense.

"I'd better go," Jeannie muttered. "Thanks for the lemon-ade." She got on her bike, pedaled down the long drive and headed for Tom and Susan's house. Already, her legs were stiff and sore. It hadn't been anything like the movie "The Black Stallion," where the boy got on the horse and almost immediately rode like the wind, not like a big bouncing awkward lump. Even her bum hurt.

Tom had gone out for the evening so she and Susan had bowls of homemade chicken noodle soup in front of the TV.

"What's the matter, honey?" Susan said. "I thought you'd enjoy your first riding lesson."

"It was okay," Jeannie muttered. She got up to go up-stairs.

"Jeannie, please take the dishes out to the kitchen and put them in the dishwasher."

Jeannie kept going as if she hadn't heard.

"Jeannie, come back here," Susan called. Jeannie ran up the stairs and into her room. A moment later, Susan knocked at the door and then came in.

She sat on the bed beside Jeannie.

"I can tell you're upset," she said. "Why don't you tell me about it and I'll see if I can help." The last thing Jeannie wanted to do was talk about how she'd made an idiot of herself this afternoon. But Susan was smiling at her and then she reached out and gently smoothed the hair off Jeannie's forehead.

"I can't ride," Jeannie said. "I'm no good at it. I'm no good at anything."

"That's not true, Arnold said you were terrific. He said you learned really fast."

"No, I'm not," Jeannie said. "I never do anything right."

"But Jeannie, you're pretty, you do well in school, you have friends here now, why do you say that?"

"Because," Jeannie said, gritting her teeth, "if I'm so smart, why did they take my mom away? I tried so hard to look after her, I did everything I could and she went away. It's all my fault." Her voice was shaking. Tears jumped out of her eyes. She buried her face in her pillow.

Susan sighed.

"Jeannie, I don't understand it very well either. You did everything you could and so did your mom. She loves you and she tried to be okay for your sake. But she needed more help than you could give her. She needed to be somewhere safe where she could rest. She's going to get better and then you can be with her again. I know that's true."

Jeannie sobbed into the pillow.

"Would you like to talk to a counselor or someone who can explain it better?"

Jeannie shook her head. The social worker had already explained everything but it didn't help.

"You don't have to go riding again if it's too hard."

"I was just scared," Jeannie said, taking her red, wet face out of the pillow. She needed to breathe and her nose was running. Susan handed her a kleenex. "It was so high up and then I fell off."

"But then you got back on. That was brave, Jeannie. I'd say you did pretty well for your first time."

"Susan and Shirley can ride way better than me."

"Susan and Shirley have been riding since they were little. They've been country kids their whole lives. You just got here. Give yourself some time to catch up."

Jeannie sat up. "I'm sorry about the dishes," she said. "I'll go do them now."

"That's okay," Susan said, "I already did them."

"Susan," Jeannie said, "can I ask you something?"

Jeannie hesitated, frowned. "Can I have some of the left-over soup?"

"Well, of course, you can have anything you want to eat. Are you still hungry?"

"It's not for me."

"It's not?"

"I saw a dog," Jeannie said shyly. "Outside, a little while ago. It seemed really hungry. I gave it some cat food."

"A stray dog!" Susan exclaimed. "That's what got into the compost. I thought there were some raccoons hanging around." Then Susan frowned. "I'll have to talk to Tom," she said. "Stray dogs can be a real nuisance. It might kill the chickens or hurt the kittens. We'll have to call someone and have it taken to the pound. Poor thing."

"It was really scared," Jeannie said. "It ran away when it saw me."

"I can't stand the idea of an animal going hungry," Susan said. "I'll fix it a bowl of food."

She and Jeannie went downstairs, and Jeannie took the bowl of food across the lawn to the shed. She put the food down, then went to feed the kittens. Susan had shown her how to pour a little milk in a bowl then dip their noses in it until they learned to drink. It made them splutter and sneeze, then they licked the milk off their noses and went sniffing around for more. Soon they were all lined up around the bowl, lapping away with their pink tongues. Jeannie picked up the black and white kitten and held it to her face. It purred and purred, turned around until it was comfortable, then fell asleep in her arms. She put it down and looked across the yard. So far, nothing had happened. The yard was quiet. Then the brown dog came slowly out of the trees, and began to creep towards the food.

Jeannie watched the dog and the dog watched her. It kept stopping but she didn't move and then it would slowly creep forward again. Finally it reached the food and began to gulp it down. Jeannie could see it more clearly now. It had long brownish yellow hair, long silky-looking ears and tail. It looked really thin.

It finished gulping the food and looked at her.

"Hey dog," she said. But this time, the dog didn't run. Instead, it wagged its tail, just a little.

"I bet you're still hungry, eh?" The dog lay down on the ground, watching her. Jeannie didn't know what to do next. She didn't know much about dogs.

"I'll bring you more food tomorrow," she said. The dog wagged its tail again, then it got up and headed for the woods.

Jeannie ran to the house.

"I saw it," she said to Susan. "I saw it. It wagged its tail. It was friendly. But it was really, really skinny."

"That's great, Jeannie," Susan said. "You sure have a way with animals. Some people are like that. Now off to bed. It's late."

Jeannie ran up the stairs to her room. Somehow, she would learn to ride, she decided, if it took her all summer, even if she fell off a hundred times, she'd figure it out.

Chapter Five

Jeannie was a very busy girl. "You keep up them marks in school," Arnold had boomed at her one day. "Don't want no bad marks hanging around my barn."

For the first time in her life, Jeannie discovered that she liked school. She spent all her lunch hours with Shannon and Shirley. It was the first time she had friends to hang around with at school. They even had their own name.

"We're the Blaze Creek gang," Shannon said. "That's 'cause we live on Blaze Creek Road and we've got our own hideout and everything."

On weekends, she spent most of her time at Arnold's. After a few more lessons, Jeannie began to feel more confident. One day, after she had ridden Billy around the corral a few times by herself, Arnold went and saddled Stony, his big Appaloosa.

"Let's go," he said, opening the gate. "Ridin' in circles is getting kind of dull for both of you." She and Billy followed Arnold and Stony up a trail behind the house. It went higher and higher until she could see far out over the valley. When Billy misbehaved, she dug in with her heels and pulled on the reins until he paid attention. Her body rocked gently as Billy walked along the trail.

"I'm riding," she thought. "I'm really riding." She was so excited by the thought that she started to say something to Arnold. Suddenly Billy jumped sideways. Jeannie pulled on the reins, squeezed with her legs, lurched over Billy's neck, but didn't fall off.

"A momma grouse," Arnold called. "Do you see it? It's pretending to be hurt to protect its babies. It's hoping we'll chase it and leave the babies alone. They'll be crouched in the grass somewhere."

The mother grouse limped down the trail in front of them, clucking loudly and dragging one of its wings. When they ignored her, she ran into the brush at the edge of the trail.

Arnold laughed. "Take good care of them babies, momma. You're a brave lady."

Farther down the trail, Arnold pointed out a mother deer with a spotted fawn at her side.

"They're not afraid of the horses," he said. "They'll let us get close." The deer moved off the trail and watched them go by. Jeannie was delighted by the tiny fawn, its flickering ears and tail, and big round eyes.

After that ride, her confidence grew and grew. Arnold even set up some jumps one day, and she and Billy practised going over them at a quick trot.

She wasn't afraid of any of the horses now, not even the bratty baby. After much consultation and giggling, they'd named him Kit Kat, because he was the same colour as a chocolate bar. Arnold said you had to be careful about the names you gave horses, because they tended to grow to be like their names. He said he figured any horse named Kit Kat was bound to be a sweetheart, and then he laughed at his own joke.

Jeannie and Shannon and Shirley went for rides beside the flashing silver river that ran at the bottom of Arnold's big pasture. Jeannie loved riding Billy. Now that he had stopped being a brat, he turned out to be well trained and gentle. She always spent lots of time brushing him and giving him treats before and after every ride.

She only had two big problems in this new life, besides missing her mother all the time. One was Caitlin, who always insisted on coming along and making a nuisance of herself. Jeannie wished that Shannon and Shirley would leave her home, but they insisted on bringing her along, put up with her tantrums, lifted her on and off the horses, and never got cranky with her. The other was the stray dog. He would let Jeannie come close but no one else could get near him. No one could catch him to take him away to the pound. Jeannie had named him Buddy, thinking about Arnold's theory of names, but so far, he wasn't anyone's friend. Every night, she took him food but she never saw him during the day.

One evening, Jeannie was just finishing her chores after supper. It was her job to take the dishes off the table and rinse and then stack them in the dishwasher. The phone rang and Susan answered.

"Jeannie, it's for you," she said.

"Hey, little one," Arnold's voice boomed in her ear. "You ever see a baby get itself born?"

"No," Jeannie said, wondering what he meant.

"Well, if you want to see something amazing, you ask your mom or dad to run you over. Tell them Bess's baby is on the way but I don't know how long it might take. Could be you won't be home until morning."

Jeannie hung up the phone, breathless with excitement. "It's Bess's baby," she said. "Arnold said I can come watch it get born. But he said it might take all night."

Tom and Susan looked at each other and nodded.

"I'll run you over there," Susan said. "Even if you have to miss a day of school, it will be worth it."

When Jeannie arrived, both Katie and Arnold were down at the barn with all the lights on. Susan fussed over Jeannie. She made sure Jeannie was wearing her warm coat and had gloves, a hat and a scarf with her.

Bess, the big black mare, was standing in the corner of her stall with her head down. Jeannie stared at her. She thought the mare looked thoughtful, as if all her energy was somehow far away and concentrated on just one thing. Katie had brought some blankets down from the house, along with a thermos of tea and some sandwiches.

"Mares always like to give birth in private," she told Jeannie. "We'll leave a light on so we can see, and we'll make ourselves comfortable in a nearby stall where she can't see us."

Jeannie helped Katie spread the blankets out on top of some clean dry hay. Then she and Arnold and Katie settled down under the blankets with Jeannie in the middle.

"We should tell some stories to pass the time," Katie said. "I'll tell one about how I first learned to ride. I was a city girl. I had just moved here and was looking for a job. I really wanted to live in the country but I didn't know much about it. I saw a job advertising for someone to help on a farm. So I went and applied. The guy who ran the place took one look at me and laughed, but he really needed help so he let me stay. He didn't have much money so he paid me almost nothing. I didn't care. I just wanted to learn about animals and gardening. He taught me a lot about taking care of animals, but he wasn't very nice. He was mean to his animals and they were all afraid of him. He had a couple of horses, a mare and her two-year-old baby. He wanted to train the baby and then sell it. That poor little horse was really afraid of him. He used to hit it to make it behave and that only made things worse. I started spending time with it, giving it treats, brushing it, letting it get to know me. A few times I slipped on its back and it didn't seem to mind.

One day, I got so mad at this guy for being mean that I yelled at him. I told him he was rude and disrespectful and mean. He was so amazed. He just stood and stared at me. I thought he was going to fire me but he didn't. He just walked away. The next day, I asked him if I could ride the colt, and he let me. We had a great time. The colt only bucked a couple of times but I managed to stay on. After that, the guy sold him to some rich person and I quit. By then, I'd met Arnold and I knew that was my real path in life."

Arnold laughed. "I've fallen off a lot of horses," he said, "but the only one that gave me a really hard time was a big old mule. I was working one time as a trail guide, taking tourists into the mountains. We liked to use mules because they are sure footed and not afraid of much of anything. I was riding this crazy mule named Applejack. He was a great mule but he just hated for anyone to get in front of him on the trail. One time, we were coming back down the mountain, and this crazy moose jumps out in front of us. The moose took off running and so did Applejack. He thought we were having a real race. I was trying to hang on and get him stopped but he wasn't paying any attention to me. Then I guess this old moose figured it was time to get lost, so he jumped over the side of the trail, and old Applejack followed right behind him. That's the point where me and Applejack parted company. I went one way and he went another, after the moose. Took me three days to find him and he was about the sorriest worest-out looking mule you ever did see."

There was a long silence. "Your turn, Jeannie," Katie said softly.

Jeannie thought hard. What could she tell a story about?

"One time my mom and me, my real mom, I mean, the one in Kelowna. My mom brought home all these boxes from behind our apartment and she said we could make our own city. We cut them up and glued them together and made them like miniature houses in our apartment. We painted them on the outside and put windows and people and cars and trees and everything on them. Some of them were big enough to sit inside so we pretended to live in there and put blankets and food in there and sometimes we even slept in them. It was really fun."

There was another long silence. Jeannie felt really embarrassed. She wondered if her story sounded silly.

"I'm sorry, I guess I kind of miss my mom," Jeannie said in a little soft voice.

"I'll bet you do," Katie said. "She sounds like a wonderful person. I liked your story a lot. You can tell us more about her if you want."

"I don't know where she is," Jeannie said. Her voice shook. "She used to be a dancer. She has long black hair.

Sometimes we'd put music on and dance together. Then one day, when I came home from school, she was gone. They said she was sick and had to go to the hospital but they didn't let me see her. The social worker just said I had to go to a foster home. I wish I could see her. I wish I knew how she was doing. I miss her so much. I used to take care of her when she was sick. She said I always made her feel better."

"Yep, I'll bet you did," Arnold rumbled.

"Susan phoned the hospital," Jeannie said. "They said she was doing okay but she still couldn't see me. I want to see her so bad. I tried to run away when I first got here, but I didn't know where to go and they wouldn't let me buy a bus ticket by myself."

"I'd do the same thing," Arnold boomed. "Any kid should have a right to see her mom."

"I wish she could see the horses someday," Jeannie said. "I wish she could see me ride."

"Well, maybe she will someday, Jeannie McBean, maybe she will. And speaking of horses, I'd better check on Bess."

He crawled out of the nest of blankets and tiptoed away. They heard a whisper. "Psst, c'mhere, you two."

They tiptoed down the corridor behind him. Bess was in the corner of the stall. She made a little low noise, like a moan, and then she lay down in the straw. She grunted again and Jeannie could see her sides heaving with effort.

"Look, here comes the baby," Katie whispered.

Suddenly, a wet black form slid out of Bess and onto the straw. Instantly, Bess got to her feet and began nosing at the baby, nickering anxiously. A wet black head with floppy wet ears raised itself out of the straw. Jeannie saw the new baby's big eyes looking around at the world. Then the foal began trying to stand up. He got his front legs under him and then promptly fell down again. He tried again and again but he kept falling over. Jeannie wanted desperately to run in and help but Katie whispered in her ear, "Just wait. He can do it. Watch now."

Bess kept licking him with her big warm tongue and talking to him in small low murmurs and whinnies. He scrambled in the straw with all four legs and suddenly heaved himself to his feet and stood there wobbling. He gave a little funny neigh, swayed and almost fell down again. Bess was still licking and smelling and checking him all over, as if he were the best present anyone could have given her. He was so funny looking. His long black ears kept flopping down. His legs were way too long for his skinny body. They kept shaking as he stood there. Then he shook his wet head and sneezed.

The baby began sniffing under his mommy's big round belly with his soft nose. It took him a few minutes but he found what he was looking for and began to nurse. The whole time he was nursing, his little black tail twitched with excitement.

"What a big strong boy," Katie crooned. "What a beautiful baby. Good girl, Bess, that's our lovely girl. Oh, I'm so proud of you." She sniffed loudly.

Jeannie looked at Katie. Tears were running down her cheeks. Jeannie felt her own eyes fill with tears.

"It's magic," Arnold said. His eyes were running too. Tears were running all over his face. "It the greatest and most wonderful moment there is, a new life coming into the world. Look at Bess. What a good mom she is. She doesn't care about the pain or effort or anything else. She just loves her baby."

The tears spilled over and ran down Jeannie's cheeks. Katie put her arms around Jeannie. "I know, sweetie," she said. "I know." And Jeannie felt that Katie really did know how sad and lonely and happy and mixed up and confused she felt, all at once. Arnold put his arms around both of them and they all stood there together, caught in the magic of the moment and the joy of the strong new life flicking its tail in the stall beside them.

Chapter Six

"No, Caitlin, get lost," Jeannie said impatiently. "You're such a pain. We're going for a long ride. We'll be gone all day. You'll get too tired."

Caitlin started to wail and looked at her big sisters for help, but they shook their heads, looking sad. Still howling, she ran off to the house. Jeannie, Shannon and Shirley got on their bikes and flew down the road to Arnold and Katie's farm. They had packed lunches for the day. They had permission from Arnold to take the horses on a trail ride up the logging roads on the mountain behind his house.

Susan had worried when Jeannie first told her of the plan. "What if you get lost?" she asked. "What if there are bears, or cougars. Can't Arnold go with you?"

Jeannie pointed out patiently that all three of them would be together, that they'd been riding all spring, that Arnold wouldn't let them go unless he thought it was safe. Actually, she was a bit scared when she thought of it. This would be a real adventure, even though they were just going up the mountain behind Arnold's house.

When they got to the farm, they caught the horses, tied them to the hitching rail, and brushed them until they shone and all the dust and loose hair was out of their coats. Then they cleaned out the horses' hooves, the way Arnold had showed them.

When the horses were clean, they carried the saddles out of the barn and each girl saddled and bridled her horse. They tied the packs with their lunches inside on the backs of the saddles. Jeannie was riding Billy, the Welsh pony. They had become good friends over the last few months. She gave him a treat and then swung easily up into the saddle. Arnold came down from the house to inspect everything and fuss over them.

"Now, remember, be back by four. Tie the horses up when you stop for lunch or they'll be back home and you'll be hoofing it. Don't run them, give them some rest when you get up high, and no goofing off and no having any darn fun or nothing, see."

He roared with laughter and slapped their horses on the rump as they started out of the yard. A logging road led up the mountain behind Arnold's house. It wound and switchbacked its way up and up through dark trees and clear patches where the trees had been cut and new baby trees were growing in the sunshine. It was June. School would be out in a couple of weeks.

"We're gonna have such a great summer," Shirley said. "We can go riding whenever we want. Or we can go to the beach. My mom takes us there in the summer when it gets too hot. We spend all day at the lake, swimming and hanging out and having picnics. It's great."

"Or we can go bike riding," added Shannon, "and there's always stuff to eat, strawberries, cherries, peaches, yum. I love summer."

It did sound pretty wonderful. Jeannie was looking forward to her first summer in the country. Summers in Kelowna were long and hot and boring. She and her mom used to go to the park and the beach a lot, or buy watermelon and sit on their balcony and eat it and spit the seeds over the railing. Jeannie remembered spending long hours reading comic books or watching stupid television programs while her mom read or drew pictures or listened to music. Sometimes they had enough money to go to a movie or rent a video but not very often.

Jeannie sighed. She had gotten a couple of letters from her mom lately, which was wonderful of course. Much better than the long silence. But the letters didn't say much. They were written on plain paper. Her mother's handwriting looked shaky and thin. The first one said only that she hoped Jeannie was well, and didn't miss her mom too much and that her foster parents were taking good care of her. After she read the first letter, Jeannie went up to her room. She sat on her bed and stared at the rug under her feet. She wrapped her arms around herself and rocked back and forth.

The letter didn't say anything. It didn't explain where her mother had gone or why. It didn't say anything about how her mother was feeling. It didn't even say that her mother missed her and loved her. Jeannie put her head down on her knees. A couple of tears squeezed their way out from under her eyelids. How could her mother write her such a stupid letter?

But the next day, Jeannie had decided perhaps her mother didn't know what to say. After all, she didn't know anything about Jeannie's new life or how she was living. So Jeannie sat down that evening and wrote her mother a long letter, telling her about Arnold and the new baby horse, about learning to ride and going logging and her new friends and how nice Tom and Susan were and how pretty her room was. Then she added how much she missed her mom, how she hoped she could see her soon. She sealed the letter and Susan promised to mail it the next day.

Jeannie waited and waited and next week there was a second letter. This one was a little longer and the handwriting was less shaky.

"Dear Jeannie: (it said) I'm feeling a little better. I miss you too. I'm so sorry I can't be with you but I'm glad you're having a good time in the country. Please be careful around the horses. Do they bite? I'm glad you have nice friends and a nice place to live. Please don't worry about me. I'm getting better. I hope I'll be able to see you soon. The doctors here have to give their permission so I can see you. I don't know when that will be. I'll be able to tell you more when I see you. I miss you so much. Remember I love you. Don't forget about me. Love, Mom."

Jeannie read this letter over and over, trying to understand. Why would her mom think Jeannie might forget about her? And why would she think that horses bite? Jeannie immediately wrote her an even longer letter, explaining all about horses, the lessons she was having at Arnold's place every weekend, how she had learned to drive Sebastien and Sally around barrels and obstacles, learned to say in a deep voice like Arnold's, "hup" and "whoa", "gee" and "haw," which meant go, and stop, right and left, and how maybe if she worked hard, she would be able to drive in the big fall horse show with Arnold. She sent this letter, but so far her mom hadn't replied. Maybe there'd be a letter Monday. Jeannie sure hoped so.

"Look," said Shannon, "look how far up we are."

Jeannie looked. They were riding along a steep rocky bank. Far below, they could see Arnold's farm, like a postage stamp farm, tiny fields and fences, black dots in the field that were the other horses grazing. There was Arnold's and Katie's house with smoke coming out of the chimney. As they watched, Arnold's old green truck went down the driveway and turned out onto the highway.

"We should give the horses a break," said Shirley. "Let's stop a while. I can see a clear space up ahead. We can stop there."

When they got to the clearing, Shannon said, "Oh look, wild strawberries," and they spent some time cramming their mouths full of the tiny bright berries. Then they lay on the grass in the sun while the horses munched grass around them. They watched the clouds for a while and talked about school, then got up and rode on.

"Wow, my stomach is complaining," said Shannon, after a while. "It's gotta be lunch time. Let's stop."

"It's not lunch yet," Shirley said. "You're always hungry. Let's wait until we get to the lunch place."

Jeannie was hungry too, but she wanted to wait until they found the perfect place for lunch. Finally they came to a place on the mountain that Arnold had told them about, a marshy pond among tall cedar trees. Someone had made a fireplace and put rough log benches around it. They tied the horses to trees and gave them some treats. Then they unpacked their lunches. Susan had packed sandwiches, a can of pop, a bag of chips, a piece of homemade carrot cake, a carton of strawberries and some yogurt. Even though it looked like a lot of food, Jeannie ate every bit. Shirley made a fire in the firepit. She and Shannon had brought wieners and marshmallows along with sandwiches, chips and home-made cookies. Jeannie managed to eat a hot dog and a couple of marshmallows on top of the rest of her lunch.

After lunch, she felt very full and very sleepy. She put her jacket down on the grass and dozed in the sun. She didn't really fall asleep. She could still hear the horses. She could hear Shannon and Shirley talking. She could hear the breeze softly rustling the cedar boughs overhead and birds singing.

After a while, Shannon came over and dropped some bits of grass on Jeannie's face. "Let's get going, sleepyhead," she laughed. "We want to get to the top today, not next week."

The horses seemed sleepy, too. They all plodded together along the trail, the horses with their heads down. Suddenly, the lead horse, River, gave a snort and jumped sideways. Shirley, who was riding in the lead, barely hung on. "Look out, a bear!" Shannon cried. The bear was running away, loping up the slope above them. The horses snorted and jumped and tried to turn around on the narrow trail and run home.

"Whoa," Jeannie yelled at Billy, who was backing up as fast as he could go. She had the reins pulled tight. "Whoa there." She was terrified he would back right over the bank and they would both fall. Then he stopped. He had backed right into a tree. The bear disappeared out of sight.

Gradually, they got the horses under control. Shirley had jumped off River and was holding tight to the reins, trying to calm him down. Shannon was leaning over Stony's neck, patting him. Jeannie jumped off Billy and checked him for scratches.

"Whew, that was scary," Shirley said.

"Yeah, we should have been watching," Shannon added. "The bear caught us all by surprise."

"Yeah, he was surprised too," Jeannie added shakily. "He sure took off in a hurry."

"Good thing he ran up the hill and not down the trail or we'd be in one big mess."

"I thought I was going to fall off for sure."

"I thought Billy was going to back right over the bank."

"I was too scared to do anything but hang on."

"Let's go back," Shirley added. "My knees are shaking. Who cares if we get to the top."

Jeannie and Shannon quickly agreed. They turned the horses around and headed back down the trail. Jeannie kept thinking about the bear. She didn't want to tell Shannon and Shirley that it was the first bear she had ever seen in her life. It had been so beautiful, wild and free. She was glad she had gotten a chance to see it. She decided as soon as she got home she would write her mother another letter and tell her all about it.

Chapter Seven

Jeannie couldn't believe how tired she was when she finally slid off Billy, back at the ranch. Her legs hurt as she unsaddled him, hung up the saddle and bridle, and then led him to the pasture to turn him loose. Shannon and Shirley looked tired too.

"And we still have to ride our bikes home and do chores," Shannon said. "I wonder if Mom would come pick us up if I sounded really pathetic on the phone."

Just then, Arnold's truck came in the yard. He jumped out of the truck and came striding towards them.

"Throw your bikes in the back of the truck, girls, and jump in," he shouted. "We got real trouble. Little Caitlin has disappeared. We need all the help we can get looking for her."

"Oh, no," Shannon and Shirley gasped together. Their faces turned white. Together they all hurried to throw their bikes into the back of Arnold's truck and then they jumped in the back as well. Katie was already in the front. They hung on tight as Arnold roared off down the drive.

When they got to Shannon and Shirley's house, there was a grim group of adults gathered in the yard. There was a police car and a tall policeman talking to Shannon and Shirley's parents.

Jeannie listened carefully. No one had seen Caitlin since this morning. At first Bonnie and James, Caitlin's parents, thought she must have tried to follow Shannon and Shirley. They phoned Arnold's house to see if she was there and discovered that the three girls had gone riding up the mountain without Caitlin. Arnold and Katie hadn't seen her. Then Bonnie decided she must be sulking somewhere on the farm and had spent an hour looking for her. She began to get scared and called James, who was shearing sheep for a neighbour. Together they had searched high and low, from one end of the farm to another. Finally, they had called the police.

Jeannie stood on the edge of the circle of excited adults. Her face was red. Her stomach hurt. This was all her fault, she thought. She hadn't wanted Caitlin along. She had been mean to her. If they'd taken Caitlin on their trail ride, this wouldn't have happened. Frantically, Jeannie tried to think. Where would she have gone if she wanted to run away and hide?

In her mind, she ran over all their favourite hiding places, the treehouse, the barn, the attic in the house. But Caitlin's parents had already looked everywhere they could think of. Caitlin must have gone somewhere unusual. Maybe she had fallen and hurt herself. Jeannie's stomach hurt even more. When everyone discovered it was her fault, they'd never talk to her again. She'd never have any friends. Everyone would think she was too mean to ever have around.

Jeannie's brain raced faster and faster. She had to find Caitlin herself, before anyone else. She had to tell her she was sorry so Caitlin wouldn't tell how mean she had been. She had to try and think like Caitlin. Where would she go if she was a little kid running away?

Suddenly, Jeannie remembered last week, when they had all been playing down by the creek. The creek was high and wild because of water running off the high mountains where the last of winter's snow was finally melting. They had had such a good time, following the creek down the mountain, throwing sticks in the water and pretending the sticks were boats, then building small dams in the mud beside the creek. They had spent a whole afternoon down there in the sun. Something about the combination of hot sun, roaring water, sand, rocks and driftwood had kept them there. Shirley and Shannon said they could all go fishing together when the water went down. Finally, they had made a kind of house out of driftwood on the sand beside a big rock before they came home. They had decided to have a picnic there when school was out. But the creek was scary and dangerous. What if Caitlin fell in?

Jeannie started to edge away from the group.

"Okay," the tall policeman was saying. "Let's all meet back here in a couple of hours. Everyone will spread out and we'll search the farm again, thoroughly. There's a search dog on the way. It'll be here in a couple of hours. Now let's get going."

Jeannie trotted off towards the edge of the trees. Behind her, someone called her name but she ignored them. It was getting late. It would soon be dark. She had to find Caitlin.

She trotted through the trees on the way to the creek. The creek tumbled down the hill beside the farm and then flattened out in a little marshy valley. There were giant cottonwood trees, a beaver dam, and long stretches of soft, golden sand where tall willow bushes grew. Jeannie hurried as fast as she could on her aching legs. A couple of times she tripped and fell, but she scrambled to her feet again and hurried on.

It was starting to get dark by the time she got to the pile of logs and driftwood which they had pretended was a house. She looked inside but there was no sign of Caitlin. She looked around the flat sandbar, dotted with brush and other piles of driftwood.

"Caitlin," she called. "Caitlin, I'm sorry. Please come home." She waited, listened with all her strength. A raven called from a nearby tree. A woodpecker rattled in the far away distance. Something tiny scuttled through the brush near her feet. But there was no sign of Caitlin.

The cold brown water in the creek roared and chewed at the creek banks. To Jeannie, it sounded angry and cruel. What if it had swallowed Caitlin somehow, eaten her up like a vicious monster? Long blue shadows had formed under the brush and trees. It was getting harder and harder to see.

"Caitlin," Jeannie called in desperation. "Caitlin." But nothing answered except the wind rattling the shiny poplar leaves together.

As Jeannie began to walk down the river, a sick feeling settled in her stomach. She was really hungry now, and cold. But that was good, she thought. She deserved to be hungry and cold while Caitlin was still missing and it was all her fault. Maybe she could just stay out here forever. If she never went back, no one could blame her for Caitlin running away.

Or maybe she would have to run away. She could hitch-hike to Kelowna somehow, and find her mother. Her mother would understand. She wouldn't blame Jeannie for wanting to have some time with her friends without Caitlin around. Jeannie's mother didn't have a lot of rules. She almost never got mad at Jeannie. That was one of the best things about her mom. Her mom always said she'd be lost without Jeannie to look after things. Jeannie knew a lot, how to find pop bottles to turn in for extra cash, what to say if the social worker called when they were on welfare, how to cook frozen perogies with lots of onions, or burritos, or canned soup with cheese sprinkled on top.

She stopped to listen again. Something crackled in the brush behind her and she jumped, suddenly terrified. What if it was a bear? If only she had a flashlight. Some brush near her shook as something rubbed against it. She opened her mouth to scream when she saw the brownish-yellow coat and sad eyes of the stray dog coming out of the brush.

Jeannie knelt on the ground.

"Buddy! C'mere, boy," she said softly. "I'm so glad to see you. I thought you were a bear." The dog wagged its tail but wouldn't come any closer. Jeannie wished she had some food for him. She wished the dog was her dog, would stay close and protect her. She patted her knee, whistled like she had heard Arnold do. The dog crawled forwards a little ways, then stopped.

"Okay," she said, "but hang around, we've got stuff to do."

Right now, she had to concentrate on the really important thing, which was finding Caitlin. She had to find her before it got so dark she couldn't see anything. What if Caitlin had to spend the night in the dark and the cold? Maybe the dog would help her find Caitlin.

"Caitlin! Caitlin!" she went on calling.

But no one answered.

Jeannie suddenly realized how exhausted she was. She was also very, very hungry. Her legs and arms ached. She had to rest. She sat down on the sand beside the creek. She put her head on her knees and stared over the rustling gurgling brown water. She sat very still. She went on sitting there, wondering what she could do next, and what she should do if they didn't find Caitlin. What if they never found her? What if she'd been kidnapped? What if a bear had gotten her? Or something worse? Jeannie's mother had always told her never to speak to strange people, never to hang around on the street or in the park by herself. She never said what might happen, but Jeannie had the idea that there were bad people out there who weren't safe to be around. She looked around but the yellow dog had disappeared again.

Suddenly, a small black head split the silver water into two lines. A round shape crawled up out of the water near her feet. It was shiny and brown, with a short tail, black ears, and a blunt nose. Jeannie sat absolutely still, hardly daring to breathe. The little animal sniffed around her feet. Then it sat up on its haunches, picked up a fallen green leaf in its front paws and stuffed it into its mouth. Jeannie remembered seeing a picture of this kind of animal in her biology book at school. It was called a muskrat. It lived in houses made of sticks out in the middle of ponds, or sometimes in tunnels in the banks of creeks.

The muskrat finished eating the grass, then sat right beside Jeannie's feet, grooming its coat with its tiny front paws. Jeannie could see its round black eyes, its whiskers, its shiny brown fur, and its black-rimmed stubby tail. Then something startled it and, in a quick movement, it slid back into the water and was gone. Buddy came out of the brush and sat beside Jeannie, still just out of reach.

Jeannie sat for a little while longer, then she got up,

determined to continue with the search. The muskrat had been so beautiful, so magical. It had felt like some kind of sign, or message. "C'mon boy," she said to the dog. "We have to keep going."

She couldn't give up now. She continued back down the creek, still calling Caitlin's name. She hated to break the silence. Her voice sounded thin and quavery when she called. Buddy followed, padding silently at her heels.

But there was still no answer, just the far-off crying of the wind through the branches of a giant cedar tree. It was funny how the wind sounded like someone crying. Jeannie stopped, listened harder. It did sound like someone crying, someone far away and scared of the dark.

"Caitlin," she screamed at the top of her lungs, "Caitlin, where are you?"

"Waaaa," said the voice. "Owwwoooo, waaaa."

Jeannie began to run in the direction she thought the voice was coming from. It was getting louder. Suddenly Jeannie saw a small dark shape huddled on the bank on the other side of the creek.

"Caitlin," she yelled. "Is that you? Are you okay?"

"Mooommmy," wailed Caitlin. "I want Moooommmy."

"Caitlin, I'm coming, I'm coming. Just wait. Hold still." Caitlin had stood up and was holding out her arms to Jeannie, still crying. Jeannie was afraid Caitlin might walk into the creek.

But how was she going to get across the creek? Then she

remembered the beaver dam. She could get across there. But it was far back up the creek.

"Caitlin, hold still. I'm coming across on the beaver dam. Just wait. I'll be right there." Caitlin hesitated, then stood still. At least she had stopped crying.

Jeannie raced with all her strength back up the creek, dodging under bushes, leaping logs, swerving around rocks. Fear and excitement had given her legs wings. She finally came to the beaver dam. It was narrow on top, made of jagged, wiggly sticks, slick with water and algae. Buddy ran out on top of the dam, leapt over the rushing water in the middle, and trotted to the other side. Jeannie began to crawl across on her hands and knees. She came to the place in the middle where the water was rushing through a hole in the top of the dam. She'd have to jump. She stood up, took a deep breath. She had to do this. The water roared and snarled at her feet like a hungry black-mouthed monster. Buddy waited on the other side, his eyes never leaving her face. She jumped with all her strength, landed on the other side of the gap, fell and caught herself, then crawled over to the other side of the dam.

She paused to gasp for breath before she took off running again, down the bank, until she came to the little patch of sand where Caitlin was standing, shivering and crying.

Caitlin's clothes were soaking wet. "I fell in the creek," she wailed, as soon as she saw Jeannie. "I'm cold. I want my Moooommmmy."

"Here," Jeannie said. She stripped off her own jacket and wrapped it around Caitlin.

"C'mon, Caitlin, I've got to get you home. Your mom and dad are so worried. Here, get on my back."

She hoisted Caitlin to her back, and began staggering towards home. She looked around for Buddy but he had disappeared again. She was afraid her legs might collapse under her but she was determined to keep going. Every so often she had to stop and rest. This side of the creek had a lot more trees and brush. It was much harder to force her way through, especially with Caitlin a dead weight on her back. Caitlin's arms were locked around her throat, making it hard for Jeannie to breathe. She could feel Caitlin shivering.

Jeannie concentrated on setting one foot in front of the other. She began counting her steps under her breath.

"Hurry, Jeannie, hurry," Caitlin said. "I'm so cold." She began to cry again.

"I am hurrying," Jeannie snapped, then she was immediately sorry for snapping at Caitlin when they were both so cold and tired.

After what seemed like an eternity of counting her footsteps, and forcing her wooden legs to take another step and another, she saw the lights of the farmhouse through the trees. She crossed the creek on the wooden bridge at the bottom of the pasture, then staggered up the lane towards the house. She had to put Caitlin down to get in the door, and when she came in, Caitlin's mother was standing by the stove, her face white and desperate.

"My baby," she screamed as soon as she saw Jeannie and Caitlin. She dropped to her knees and Caitlin ran into her arms. They held onto each other for a while, then Bonnie stood up and came over to Jeannie.

"Oh, Jeannie," she said. "How can I ever thank you enough? Where did you find her? Oh, goodness, I've got to call everybody. How can I call them? And Caitlin's so cold and wet. Oh, and you must be so hungry. Everyone will be starving." She gave Jeannie a huge hug then went back and held on to Caitlin again. Finally, she seemed to pull herself together.

Bonnie ran outside and clanged the big bell that hung on the porch. Then she ran back inside, stripped off Caitlin's wet clothes, ran a hot bath and got Caitlin into it. All of her movements were fast, as if she were afraid if she didn't get everything done at once, get Jeannie and Caitlin warm and fed and looked after, they'd both disappear again. She dished Jeannie a bowl of soup from the big pot of soup simmering on the stove. Jeannie had sunk into a chair by the kitchen table. The kitchen was so warm and smelled so good. It made her feel sleepy. She ate the soup then put her head down on her arms.

Footsteps banged on the back porch and people began arriving, their excited voices asking question after question, but Jeannie was so tired, she could only mumble a response.

She couldn't quite keep track of what was happening. Arnold and Katie were there, and the tall policeman who kept asking her questions. Then Susan and Tom showed up and finally she was home in her own warm soft bed; everything was all right again and she could let herself sink into the soft mattress and into the soft warm arms of sleep.

But just before she fell asleep, she thought again of that magical dark moment, when the muskrat had sat at her feet, chewing a piece of grass. She thought of the sad wild dog, with his dark eyes and timidly wagging tail She thought that someday she would like to do that again, sit very quietly on the bank of the creek, so quiet that the life of the plants and animals would go on as if she weren't even there. She could learn about them and, for a short while, even be a part of their lives.

Chapter Eight

The next day was Sunday. Jeannie slept in and woke to the delicious smell of bacon frying. She looked at the clock beside her bed. It was late, after 10 o'clock. She got up, dressed, and ran down to the kitchen. Susan and Tom were making pancakes, cooking bacon and eggs. There was maple syrup and three kinds of jam, fresh squeezed orange juice, a platter of fruit. There was whipped cream and strawberries.

"Come and sit down, honey," Susan said. She came over and gave Jeannie a big hug. "We want to celebrate. We're so proud of you. We think you're a real hero and so does everybody else. The phone has been ringing all morning but we didn't want to wake you up. Caitlin's parents phoned to see how you were doing, and the reporter from the local paper wants to interview you."

Jeannie slipped into a chair. She was so hungry. Tom came around the table and gave her a hug as well. "You're one terrific girl, Jeannie Mcleod," he said. Jeannie looked at Tom in surprise. Usually he didn't say too much. She had thought to herself a few times that probably this whole foster child thing was pretty much Susan's idea and that Tom was just going along with it. Tom's thin face had a huge grin on it. He was wearing a denim shirt and clean blue jeans. He looked really nice, Jeannie thought. Susan was wearing a long skirt, a white blouse, and her brown hair was, for once, hanging loose around her face. Jeannie thought she looked really pretty that way. Also, for once, neither she nor Tom looked worried. Their faces were relaxed and shining.

"You know, Jeannie," Susan said, her voice suddenly very serious. "Tom and I should have told you before, but we weren't sure what to say. We just wanted to let you know that it's been wonderful having you here. You've brought a lot of happiness into our lives."

"That's right, Jeannie," Tom nodded. "I wasn't sure, at first, just how it was going to work out, but it's been a real pleasure, young lady, all the way. Now enough speechmaking. Let's eat."

Jeannie dished up a huge pile of pancakes, strawberries, whipped cream, and covered the whole thing with maple syrup. Then she had several pieces of bacon and scrambled eggs. She had two glasses of orange juice and sat back, full at last.

"Since today's a day of celebration, we thought we could do something together." Tom said. "Maybe a walk, a picnic, drive to the beach, come back, pick up some videos, have the whole day together. What do you think, Jeannie?"

Jeannie hesitated. She felt like she still didn't know Tom and Susan that well. Between school and hanging out at Arnold and Katie's, or Shannon and Shirley's, she hadn't spent that much time at home. But she also knew she was too embarrassed to go to Arnold's, or Shannon and Shirley's house. They were all thinking she was some kind of hero. What if they knew that the whole mess with Caitlin was her fault? Would any of them ever speak to her again? It was bad enough to fool Tom and Susan, to not say anything to them.

She nodded her head. "That'd be nice," she said. Tom and Susan smiled as if she had just given them a whole bunch of birthday and Christmas gifts all rolled up into one terrific package.

"Grab your bathing suit and a towel, sweetheart," Susan said, coming over to hug her yet again. "I'll pack some snacks, or we can eat at the beach. They have the greatest hot dogs there. Or we can stop along the way. Whatever you want, Jeannie."

"I'll clean the car and bring along that rubber dinghy we bought last year," Tom shouted, on his way out the door.

"Yahoo! We'll finally get a chance to use it." He jumped in the air like a little kid and slapped his hand against the roof of the porch.

Jeannie was amazed. Tom and Susan were acting like kids just let out of school. She felt guiltier than ever. She didn't dare tell them she was no hero, just someone who had made a bad mistake and then tried to make up for it.

Jeannie had one of the best days she could ever remember. Tom and Susan sang silly songs all the way to the beach in the car, and taught them to Jeannie and finally got her to join in. At the beach, she and Tom tried to row the rubber dinghy but it kept going around in circles and they giggled so much they tipped it over, then all three of them got in a contest of who could tip the other one out of the boat. When they were cold and shivering, they lay on the sand in the sun, toasting themselves. When they were hot and sleepy, they wandered up to the hot dog stand and stuffed themselves on hot dogs and french fries and milkshakes. Jeannie couldn't believe she was so hungry again after her huge breakfast. Then they all had a nap under the beach umbrella. When they woke up, they went for another swim, then slowly packed up to go home. On the way home, they stopped and rented three comedy videos. Once they were home, Susan made an enormous bowl of very buttery popcorn and they ate it with hot chocolate with tiny multi-coloured marshmallows on top. Jeannie fell asleep halfway through the second video and was only dimly aware of Tom carrying her up to bed, of Susan undressing her, tucking her in, and kissing her goodnight.

"Night Susan, night Tom," she murmured sleepily. Then she remembered and sat up again. "I have to feed Buddy," she said. "I forgot. He came when I was in the woods, looking for Caitlin. He came and protected me. I have to take care of him."

"Don't worry," Tom said. "I'll put out some food. Maybe one day he'll learn to trust us too."

"Good night, sweetheart," they both said, turned out the light, and tiptoed out of the room.

Chapter Nine

Jeannie dreaded going to school the next day but it turned out okay. Everyone was friendly but no one made too big a fuss. There were a few jokes about her being the big hero, but nothing mean. Her teacher smiled warmly at her and even the principal said, "Hi Jeannie," with an extra big grin when she saw Jeannie in the hall. Jeannie got her picture in the paper which was pretty embarrassing. Susan taped a clipping of it to the fridge. After a while, everyone forgot about Jeannie in their excitement that school was almost finished. Kids were talking about their plans for summer, about going fishing, going to summer camp, going to the beach, going on trips with their families.

Finally the last day of school came. Jeannie went over to

Shannon and Shirley's after school. Jeannie hadn't been there for a while. She still felt guilty, but she didn't know what to do about it. When she came in the house, Caitlin was in the hall. She decided she had better say something right away.

"Caitlin," she said in a low voice, "I'm sorry I wouldn't let you go riding with us. I'm sorry I yelled at you. I know you were mad at me. Please don't ever run away again, okay? I won't be mean to you again."

"You're mean," Caitlin said. "You're always mean to me."

"I said I was sorry. I'll try and be nicer, okay?"

"I want to go riding with you," Caitlin demanded. Jeannie sighed.

"Sure," she said. "I'll take you riding. I'll even ask Arnold if you can ride on the wagon sometime."

Caitlin smiled.

"You know why I ran away? I was mad at Mommy. She made me go outside. She said I was a whiny spoiled brat. So I went down to the creek to play house. Only I fell in and then I ended up on the other side and I couldn't get back."

"Caitlin, you might have drowned," Jeannie cried.

"I can swim good," Caitlin said scornfully. "But it was really, really cold. I was so cold, Jeannie, but then you came, so it was okay."

So now Jeannie had nothing to feel guilty about. The summer shone before her, clean and golden and contented. Except for her mother, stuck in a hospital somewhere in stupid Kelowna.

"Susan, why is mom still in the hospital? Why doesn't she get better?" Jeannie asked that night, as Susan was tucking her into bed. They had begun to have long chats after school and at night before bed. Jeannie discovered that Susan was pretty easy to talk to, even though she worried about everything too much.

Susan sighed. "It's her illness, Jeannie. It's difficult. Sometimes it takes people a while to recover Sometimes people call it depression, or manic depression, or bipolar disease. I don't know that much about it, just some things I read. But I know your mom tried very hard to look after you and keep it all together. I guess after a while it all got to be too much. She had what they call a psychotic episode. That's a big word meaning she got really mixed up about what was real and what wasn't. She's getting better now though. She's seeing a therapist. They're trying to find the right medication. They have to keep trying different things until they find the one that works. And when they do, she'll be able to go home. People with your mom's illness do fine when they get the right treatment. I don't know when you can see her. Soon, I hope."

"I wrote her another letter," Jeannie said. "I told her all about the trail ride and the bear and Caitlin getting lost and our trip to the beach and Buddy the dog. I hope she writes back soon."

And the next day, lying on the kitchen table, was another letter from Jeannie's mom.

"Dear Jeannie," it said, "your letters are like beautiful stories. They make me so happy. You write so well. I can't really picture everything because I don't know much about the country. But it sounds so beautiful. I try to imagine pictures to go with your stories. Maybe you could send me some drawings or photographs sometime. The doctors say I am getting better. They have finally found some medicine that seems to work. I miss you so much. I keep dreaming about the time when we can be together again. I was afraid to tell you that earlier, because I thought it might make you sad. But now I am beginning to think we can be together again soon. I am so grateful to Tom and Susan for taking such good care of you. Someday, I hope to be able to thank them myself. Please be careful around the horses. I'm afraid they might hurt you. All my love. Mom."

Jeannie took the letter up to her room. She sat on the bed with the letter in her hand. She missed her mom so much her throat closed tight and hard with the wanting. She missed her so much she wanted to run out of the room, down the stairs, down the road, as hard as she could run, all the way to her mother's lap and her mother's arms.

When Susan came upstairs, Jeannie was curled in a tight ball of misery on the bed. Susan sat down and rubbed her back. Jeannie turned over and sat up. Susan wrapped Jeannie in her arms and they sat together without speaking, rocking gently back and forth.

"I want to see her so bad," Jeannie said. "I just want to

know she's okay. I just want her to tell me she's feeling okay."

"I understand," Susan said. "I will phone the hospital and try to get permission for you to have a visit. If your mom is feeling better, there's no reason why you can't see her. Come on downstairs. We'll phone right now."

Downstairs, Susan dialed the hospital while Jeannie waited.

"Yes, I'm Susan Anderson. I'm calling on behalf of Jeannie Mcleod. She's our foster daughter. She wants to know how her mother is doing and when she can see her."

Susan waited patiently, not saying much. She repeated the same story to someone on the other end two more times. Finally, she said, "Okay, thank you," and hung up.

She turned to Jeannie and said, "Her doctor will call us later. They didn't tell me anything. We'll just have to wait."

Then she looked at Jeannie's sad face and said, "Big hospitals are always like that. It takes time to get through all the channels. Don't worry. They'll call soon."

Jeannie went upstairs and lay on the bed, waiting. The phone kept ringing. Every time it rang, Jeannie tensed up, waiting for Susan to call her. But it wasn't until after lunch that the phone rang and Susan called Jeannie, excitement in her voice. "Jeannie, come quick. It's your mother."

Jeannie flew down the stairs and grabbed the phone. "Mom?" she said hesitantly.

"Hello, Jeannie," said a soft familiar voice. "I'm so sorry I haven't been able to call."

Tears gathered in Jeannie's eyes and spilled down her cheeks. "Mom, where are you?" she cried.

"I'm still in the hospital," her mother said, "but I'm hoping I'll be out by September. Then maybe we can start over, get our lives together. But you sound so happy there, Jeannie. Are you sure you want to come back here?"

"I want to be with you, Mom," Jeannie said.

"That's what I want too," her mother said. "But I have to be sure I'm okay."

"Mom, what happened? Where did you go? I came home and all those police were there. And then the social worker came."

"I don't really remember, Jeannie. I was pretty out of it around that time, don't you remember?"

Jeannie did remember. It had been one of those times when she would come home to find her mother curled up in a chair or in bed. Jeannie would make her mother some tea and a sandwich, coax her to eat, turn on the TV and seat her mother in front of it. She knew if she waited long enough, her mother would come back from wherever she was, smile and hug Jeannie and be herself again. She just had to wait. That's what she'd been telling herself even though it scared her when her mother wouldn't talk or look at her, just stared straight ahead into some dark place that Jeannie was excluded from. She had to do all the shopping and cooking and cleaning herself during those times. She had learned to get by on canned soups and frozen stuff that could be heated in the oven. The worst times were when she ran out of money and she couldn't get her mother to go to the bank. Sometimes they had no money and they just had to wait for the welfare cheque to come in the mail. Then Jeannie would get by on whatever scraps of food she could find in the apartment but her mother wouldn't eat at all.

"It wasn't so bad," Jeannie said. "We were doing okay."

"Jeannie, we'll talk about it some other time," her mom said. "Right now, I can't stay on the phone for very long. My doctor wants to talk to you and then I have to go. Write me another letter, please, honey, and tell what you're doing for the summer. I love your letters. They make me so glad you're okay. Bye darling. I love you so much. I miss you so much. Gotta go."

"But Mom . . ." Jeannie said.

Then another voice came on the line, a man's deep voice.

"Hi, Jeannie," said the voice. "We've never met. I'm Dr. Thornton."

"I want to talk to my mother," Jeannie said stubbornly.

"Your mother is a little tired right now. She can't come to the phone because she's going to have a rest," the voice said. "I just wanted to tell you she's doing really well, and as soon as we can arrange it, we'd like you to come for a visit. Would you like that?"

"Yes, please," said Jeannie. She could hear the smooth power in this man's voice. She decided to be very careful about what she said. This man could change her life.

"Okay then, I'll let your foster parents know when it's time. Take good care of yourself, Jeannie."

The phone clicked in her ear. Slowly she hung up and went and sat at the kitchen table, laying her head on her arms. Susan came and sat beside her. They sat there together for a little while. Finally, Jeannie sat up.

"Can I go over to Arnold's now?" she asked. "I think I'd like to go riding or maybe just hang out with the horses."

"Sure," Susan said. "I'll see you for supper. Don't be late. We're having strawberry shortcake."

Jeannie pedaled her bike the three miles to Arnold's farm. No one was around. Arnold and Katie had gone to town for groceries. The horses were all standing in a big group in the corner of the pasture, in the shade of a clump of maple trees. Billy was lying down, stretched out on a patch of grass. Jeannie lay down beside him, pillowing her head on his warm satiny neck. He gave a long sigh to acknowledge her existence. They lay there together in the warm and sleepy afternoon sun. Jeannie didn't care if her clothes got dusty and covered in grass seeds.

"Billy," she said softly, "I'm going to see my mom. I'm finally going to see her." She had to tell somebody. He flicked an ear at her and sighed deeply and she scratched his chest gently while the sun warmed both of them.

She tried to remember every detail of her mother. Her mother always wore sweaters and blue jeans. Her black hair was usually long and caught in a pony tail. Her eyes were brown. Sometimes she looked so tired and worried, especially when she and Jeannie had to move again. Sometimes she would cry at night when she thought Jeannie was asleep. Other days she was so happy. Jeannie loved it when her mom was happy. She would make up stories to tell Jeannie. Her mom was such a good storyteller.

Jeannie wanted to ask her mom so many questions. What had happened to the rest of their family? Why didn't they have a family the way everyone else did? Did she have a dad somewhere or a grandma? What had really happened that terrible day when Jeannie came home from school and found her mom gone? And how could they keep it from ever happening again?

Chapter Ten

"MOM!" Jeannie yelled. Her mother was coming towards her down the hospital corridor. At last. Jeannie flung herself down the long hall and into her mother's arms. Susan and Tom stood watching, smiling.

"Oh my, Jeannie," said her mother. "You're so tall, and brown, and grown up. My goodness, you've changed."

"This is Tom and Susan, Mom," Jeannie said. "This is my mom, Judy Mcleod." Then Jeannie's mom introduced Doctor Thornton, who was hovering anxiously on the edge of the group as if he were checking on everyone. Jeannie resented him. She wished he would go away. Her mother seemed thin and nervous. Her hair was cut short, which made her look strange. Her eyes kept going from person to person, as if she weren't quite sure what they were doing there. Jeannie kept staring at her mother as if she were afraid she would disappear. She pressed in close to her mother's side and hung on tight to her hand. Her mom's hand felt so familiar. It felt like something safe to hang onto. Even her smell was familiar. Jeannie pushed her face against her mother's arm.

"Why don't we all sit down?" Dr. Thornton said, ushering them into a nearby waiting room. He was wearing a suit and tie. He was very tall and thin with grey hair. He looked as though he worried a lot. The waiting room had orange plastic chairs, dull yellow linoleum, dull yellow walls. They all sat down, Jeannie beside her mother, still gripping tightly to her hand.

Dr. Thornton took over immediately, talking as if he were in charge of everything and nobody else had anything to say.

"This is a very important meeting," he said, in his big booming voice.

Oh yeah, like we can't figure that out, Jeannie thought impatiently to herself.

"It's a good idea that we are all in clear communication with each other," Dr. Thornton went on. "I'm sure we all want the same thing, for Judy here to feel better and to be able to spend some time with Jeannie as a family. I'm sure we all want to be part of the team and cooperate so everything will be for the best."

What's he talking about? Jeannie thought.

"Jeannie, you know your mom hasn't been feeling very well, and now that she has begun her recovery, it's important that she gets lots of rest and nothing disturbs that process. It's going to be a while before we can do an assessment to make sure that a stable family unit here is the best outcome of this program."

"When is my mom going to be okay? When can we be together?" Jeannie interrupted rudely.

There was sudden silence. Everyone looked at Jeannie.

"That's what I've been trying to explain," Dr. Thornton continued. "Your mom is doing great but we still have a ways to go. The important thing is that we all stay in touch and continue to enhance smooth communication, so that whatever happens is the very best thing for everyone concerned."

Jeannie looked at her mom. Her mom winked at her and gave her a small secret grin. Suddenly Jeannie felt a whole lot better. Dr. Thornton wasn't so bad. He just talked funny.

"Now maybe we could get some coffee and leave Jeannie and her mother to visit," said Dr. Thornton. Susan and Tom left with Dr. Thornton. Jeannie leaned against her mother. She wanted to crawl into her lap and stay there for a long time. The two of them sat there holding onto each other.

"Tom and Susan seem really nice," Jeannie's mother said after a while.

"Everybody's been great," Jeannie said. "I wish you could

meet them, especially Arnold and Katie, and all the horses . . . and Shannon and Shirley and Caitlin. We're going to the beach tomorrow." She stopped, feeling guilty, because her mother couldn't go to the beach. She was stuck inside these dull walls where the sun never shone at all.

"Jeannie, I've been thinking," her mom said. "You're having such a good life, much better than you ever had with me. I know it's hard but it's better that you stay with Tom and Susan for a while. When I think about all those dumpy apartments we used to live in, it gives me the creeps. I'm so glad you're somewhere having a good time and learning so much."

"But Mom, I want to live with you," Jeannie shouted. She started to cry. She put her head down to hide her eyes but she couldn't stop the sniffling sounds coming from her nose. She hated to cry in front of her mother.

"Yes, my darling, we will when things get better," her mother said. She patted Jeannie's back. "Until then, we just have to be patient. I know it's hard for you to understand what's going on. But I need some time to think and plan. I want things to be better for us in the future. I have to think about what to do next. Maybe I can get some money to go back to school. But Dr. Thornton says I just have to wait until he's sure the drugs I take are working. I keep trying to be patient but you know I'm not very good at it. I like it when things are more exciting." She stood up and began to pace back and forth. "Jeannie, it's hard for me to be here, but at least I know what to expect, and I don't have to cook or look after anyone, just myself. I want what's best for you, don't you know that?"

Judy was talking very fast and pacing back and forth. Jeannie watched her. "You'll have to wait," she went on, "until I get everything together. I've still got a lot of getting better to do, Jeannie. It's good for me to know you're being looked after. I just can't manage to be your mother right now. I can't look after both of us. I just can't. Do you understand that? I can't do it." She kept pacing back and forth.

Jeannie sat on the couch crying and trying not to cry. Her throat hurt as if it were on fire. She felt so lonely, lonelier than she had ever been in her life. She wished her mom would come and sit down and hold her and tell her everything was going to be all right. Instead, Dr. Thornton and Susan and Tom came back; then it was time to go. Jeannie hugged her mother, but she felt as if she were being torn in two.

All the way back to Tom and Susan's house, she sat in the back seat of the car, staring out the window and wondering what she was going to do now. The visit with her mother had been too fast. It had left more questions in Jeannie's head than it had answered. Jeannie knew what she wanted, she wanted to be with her mother. She knew her new life was more wonderful than anything she could ever have dreamed of. But it couldn't replace the bond between herself and her mom. Nothing would ever replace that.

Then she thought about her mother pacing back and forth, talking so fast, how strange her eyes had looked. Sometimes it felt to Jeannie like her mom was two people, Mom and someone else, someone really scary that Jeannie didn't understand at all. And that made her feel even lonelier than before, even when she was spending time with her mom.

Chapter Eleven

"We've got to do something about Buddy," Tom said. "One of the neighbours told me he took a shot at a stray dog that was after his chickens. If we don't manage to gain Buddy's trust, and teach him how to behave, someone will shoot him. You can't have a stray dog where there's cows and chickens. If we can't catch him, I'll have to call the wildlife officers."

"What will they do to him?" Jeannie asked.

"They'll try and trap him and take him to the SPCA, who'll find him a home," Tom said.

"But he likes me," Jeannie said.

"Jeannie, you have such an amazing way with animals," Susan said, "but he won't come near Tom or me. I've called him and taken food to him. He just runs away."

"What can we do?" Jeannie said.

"Maybe you should talk to Arnold," Susan suggested. "He knows about training animals. Maybe he'll have an idea."

Arnold did have some ideas, so, that night, when it was time to feed Buddy, Jeannie tried to do what Arnold had suggested. She put the food bowl on the ground and sat down beside it. She sat very quietly, just as she had been sitting when the muskrat came.

Buddy came out of the brush at the side of the lawn. He wagged his tail when he saw her, then he came trotting forward to get his food. But he stopped, just out of Jeannie's reach, too far away from the bowl to reach the food, when he saw her looking at him. She put out her hand and he backed away.

Deliberately, Jeannie turned her head away and stared across the yard at the house. Arnold said animals didn't like to be stared at. He had told Jeannie to give Buddy time to learn to trust her. She heard Buddy begin to crunch at the dog food. Finally he stopped.

She felt a gentle sniff on the back of her neck. She stayed quiet. Buddy sniffed at her hair, her clothes, her feet, her hands. Then very abruptly, he yawned and lay down beside her. She yawned and lay down too. He turned his head to look at her. She closed her eyes and ignored him.

She felt him sniffing her cheek. Then he licked it gently with his pink tongue. Jeannie couldn't help herself. She laughed. "Buddy, that tickles," she said. Buddy backed away but not far.

She sat up and he sat up too. She put out her hand and he sniffed it, then licked it all over. She reached up and scratched behind his ears, along his neck and back. When she stopped, he leaned against her, asking for more. Jeannie felt tears in her eyes. Buddy had been so lonely, like her. He just needed a friend he could trust.

She sat with him for a long time on the dark lawn. When it was time to go in, he followed her to the door, then curled up outside it. He was still there when she came out in the morning.

"Look's like you've got yourself a dog," Tom said the next morning, laughing.

Jeannie and Buddy were playing soccer, or at least Jeannie was trying to play soccer, but Buddy kept stealing the ball. He still wouldn't let Tom or Susan pet him but at least he didn't run away.

"It'll take a little time," Arnold said, when she phoned him. "Just be patient. Buddy's been a wild dog for a long time. Maybe someone hurt him real bad in his life and he has to learn to trust people all over again, one at a time. But he'll come around. When a dog decides to be your dog, he'll be loyal the whole rest of his life. That's something you can depend on."

The rest of the summer swooshed by like a galloping horse. Jeannie had a new adventure almost every day. She went riding a lot and she practised driving the team with Arnold. Now that Buddy had made up his mind to be Jeannie's dog, he never left her side. He made friends with the horses and soon learned to ride in the wagon with Jocko.

Jeannie learned to guide Sebastien and Sally around obstacles, through gates, in circles and figure eights. She couldn't believe there had ever been a time in her life that didn't include horses, the feel of horses, the smell of horses, the sounds of horses. She had learned so much, how to clean and brush their thick coats, how to pick up their feet and clean the mud out from under their heavy metal horse-shoes, how to slip the bits in their mouths and the bridles over their huge heads and soft ears, how to slap them on the shoulder and say briskly, "Get over there," when she needed them to move, how to back them into the wagon shafts so Arnold could hitch them up. She had also learned to be very careful around the horses. They were so big that any carelessness could cause trouble. Sebastien had accidental-ly stepped on her foot one day and she limped around with a badly bruised foot for a week. He had waggled his ears and looked very sorry when she yelled at him, but now she remembered to keep her own feet out of his way.

After practice, she would help lift off the heavy sweaty harness, which all had to be cleaned and wiped off later. She brushed the horses, cleaned their feet again, and gave them treats before turning them loose in the pasture. Arnold laughed one day when he saw her leading the two huge horses behind her.

"You look like the mouse leading the elephants," he laughed, and from that day on, he called her various nicknames, such as "wee mousie," and "Jeannie the mouse," "mouse girl," and sometimes, "elephant woman." Jeannie no longer minded his nonsense. She loved the gentle way he handled the horses, the soft stern voice he used when he wanted them to do their best. He made fun of things and he could always find something to laugh at, but he could be very serious too. She liked that.

When she wasn't with the horses, she played with Shannon and Shirley, or went places with Tom and Susan. One day Tom and Susan borrowed a van and took Jeannie, Shannon, Shirley, Caitlin, Luke and Jason to a waterslide park. Afterwards, they all went for hamburgers and ice cream and came home exhausted but happy.

One day, Tom, Susan, Arnold and Katie all went hiking together in the mountains. They found some huckleberries to pick and went fishing for brook trout in a rushing mountain stream, then cooked them for lunch over a campfire. Jeannie thought how much easier it was to ride a horse up the mountains than drag herself up them on foot.

But the summer went by all too quickly. Jeannie continued to write long letters to her mom. Tom and Susan took her to Kelowna now twice a month to visit her mother. It took an hour to drive there. These visits were never enough and never long enough. It felt as though Jeannie and her mother barely got time to talk before some nurse or doctor came in and the visit was over again. The visits were a lot better than nothing, but it wasn't the same as having her mother to herself all the time.

One day, Jeannie was eating breakfast when Susan said, "Jeannie, we have to plan a time to go shopping for new school clothes and supplies. School will be starting in two weeks."

Jeannie sat there in shock. Two weeks! She wasn't ready to go back to school. She wanted the summer to go on forever. Oh no, she thought, locked up in school again.

Susan laughed. "Jeannie, don't look so upset. School won't be so bad. You get to see all your friends. And you do so well in school. You'll have fun this year because you know everybody and you'll just be part of the gang. We'll get you some great new clothes, a new backpack, maybe a new Walkman, would you like that?"

"Sure," said Jeannie, but her heart sank. Somehow, she had thought that when school started, she would be living with her own mother again. In her head, she had pictured them in a beautiful new apartment, maybe with a car so they could come for visits to Tom and Susan's house. She had pictured introducing her mother to all her new friends, showing off riding horses, driving the team. She had pictured taking her mother on a ride in the wagon, and how impressed her mother would be.

And she wanted to show Shannon, Shirley, Luke and Jason that her mother was as normal as anyone else. Nobody said much to her, but she realized that the other kids knew her mom was in the psych ward. Jason had asked her one day, "So, is your real mom crazy or what?"

"She's not crazy," Jeannie said fiercely. "She just needed some time to rest. She's fine. I'm going to be living with her soon." She clenched her fists.

Shannon and Shirley came and stood beside her. "Hey, you leave her alone," they said to Jason. "You're just mean. He's a creep, Jeannie, don't pay any attention to him."

Nobody else said anything to her about her mother. That bothered her too. She wanted to talk about her mother but it was as if her real mother were invisible. Her friends all referred to Tom and Susan as her mom and dad, and now, gradually, Jeannie had started calling them that too.

It didn't seem strange to her to have two mothers. They were so different. And since she had never had a dad, it was really fun to hang out with Tom, help him with chores, or watch while he fixed things around the house. And she had Arnold to talk to as well. Jeannie thought that if she ever did have a dad, she'd want him to be like Arnold.

She and Susan had long talks about things. Susan was showing Jeannie how to cook. They would sit in the kitchen in the morning, before the day got too hot, talking about everything under the sun. Susan would be peeling apples for a pie, or mixing bread dough, or chopping onions for soup. She was always busy at something. She sat on a stool at the edge of the kitchen table, while Jeannie watched her and helped by tasting, munching, or fetching knives, pots or pans, or sometimes ingredients out of the cupboards.

But today Jeannie didn't feel like doing anything. She tried to think about going shopping but all she could think about was another long time spent without her mother. Instead of helping Susan, she went upstairs and lay on her bed. She lay there and thought of all the things she should be doing but she didn't feel like doing any of them. She curled up in the middle of her bed, holding onto her black and white kitten which was curled up beside her on the bed, purring. She felt too sad even to cry. She thought about her mother, lonely in the ugly yellow rooms of the hospital. Jeannie wished she could phone her. When Susan called her for lunch, she yelled down that she wasn't hungry, then slammed the door of her room shut. Susan came up the stairs and knocked on her door.

"Are you okay, Jeannie?" she said, in her soft voice. "Are you sick? Do you want some aspirin?"

"I don't want anything," Jeannie said. "I just want to be alone." She petted the kitten, which licked her hand with its pink tongue.

Susan went away again. Jeannie could hear her talking to Tom in the kitchen, but she couldn't hear what they were saying. After a while, she could hear Tom coming up the stairs. She could tell because his footsteps were heavier and slower than Susan's.

"Jeannie," said Tom's deep voice. "I just wanted to let you know I'm going to be taking the new pots out of the kiln this afternoon. If you want to help me, that would be great."

Jeannie didn't say anything and after a while, she could hear Tom's footsteps going back down the stairs. Jeannie went on lying on her bed, feeling sad. She really wanted to see Tom's new pots come out of the kiln. It was so exciting to see the brown clay shapes transformed into wonderful jars, bowls, plates, cups and saucers. Later, Jeannie knew, he would take them to the craft shop in the town. Jeannie had gone with him a couple of times and had loved looking at all the wonderful things in the craft store, stained glass boxes, embroidered pillows, soft woven shawls, wooden toys. It was one of her favourite places to visit. She had even used some of her money from Arnold to buy her mother a present, a small silver necklace of a galloping horse.

The afternoon went on. Jeannie could smell the wonderful smell of apple pie fresh from the oven. Her stomach began to rumble and feel very empty. After a while, it began to ache. Jeannie thought of all the good food waiting downstairs. Still she didn't move.

She heard the back door slam. She got up and looked out the window. Susan was going down the driveway with Tom. They were holding hands and looked as though they were going for a walk. Then Jeannie remembered. Susan had told her that morning that they were all going for a visit to see one of their neighbours who had just bought a new grand piano. Susan had even suggested that Jeannie might want to try taking piano lessons. The neighbours were a couple of people who had just finished buying some property and building a new house. They both played music. One played the piano and one played the guitar and fiddle. Susan said they were going to have music nights next winter. Everyone in the community would bring food, musical instruments, and entertain themselves and each other.

Finally, Jeannie couldn't stand it any longer. Her stomach was demanding that she put something in it. She got up and went down the stairs. There was a piece of pie and a glass of lemonade on the kitchen table. Beside the food was a note with her name on it. The note read, "Hope you're feeling better. Enjoy the pie. We've gone to the neighbours for a visit. Love, Tom and Susan."

Jeannie sat at the table. She ate the pie and drank the lemonade. Her stomach felt a lot better. She looked in the fridge. There was some leftover barbecued chicken. She got the bread and made herself a chicken sandwich with lots of mayonnaise, salt and pepper. Then she had some more lemonade. Finally, she had another piece of pie.

When she went in the bathroom and looked in the mirror, she could see that her face looked dirty, her hair was sticking up in odd places. She combed her hair, washed her face, and went outside to sit in the sun. Buddy ran frisking and wagging his tail to sit beside her and put his head in her lap to be petted. She rubbed his silky ears and he rolled on his back in the sun.

She didn't feel so terrible anymore. The longing and aching for her mother had subsided, at least for a little while. When Tom and Susan came home, she and Buddy ran to meet them, and together they walked up the driveway, Jeannie in the middle, holding on to each of their hands.

Chapter Twelve

"Hang on, Jeannie McBean," Arnold shouted. "Here we go. Hup, hup, Seb, Sal, let's go, team!" It was the opening parade for the big Draft Horse Show which was held every year in late September in Sandpoint, Idaho. Arnold had been getting ready for weeks, and Jeannie had been helping on weekends and after school. Now here they were, dressed in shiny new denim pants and shirts, real cowboy hats on their heads, new cowboy boots on their feet, entering the ring with a lot of other horses and wagons. Sebastien and Sally lifted their ponderous great hooves and lowered their great heads. Jeannie thought they were the most beautiful team in the whole show, but she had to admit, most of the other teams were pretty impressive.

Some of the teams were made up of six giant horses matched in colour.

Jeannie knew the different breeds of heavy horses now. There was a team of giant matched black Clydesdales, and a team of six matched light brown Belgian horses. There was another team of grey Percherons, like Sebastien and Sally, and a team of six matched mules. Some of the wagons were pulled by little ponies, dressed up with ribbons braided into their manes and tails. Jeannie was fascinated by it all. Her head kept swiveling from side to side. There was so much to see.

At the head of the parade were riders on riding horses, their saddles and bridles decorated with silver. The riders, beautifully dressed, were carrying the flags of the USA, Canada, Idaho, and British Columbia.

As they circled around the ring together, the people on the other wagons waved and smiled. Everyone was so friendly. Everyone knew Arnold, and Jeannie felt instantly at home with them all. Even though people were competing against one another, everyone helped out, and everyone was interested in how well other people were doing. Jeannie had been giving Sebastien a bath with a hose last night, when a girl her own age from one of the other wagons came over and helped hold him still. The girl lived far away, in Montana. She said they came to the horse show every year. Her name was Norma Jean; she and Jeannie laughed over the resemblance in their names.

Jeannie, Katie and Arnold had come to the horse show in a huge truck with the wagon in the back and the horses in a horse trailer behind that. It took them all day to drive to Sandpoint. They had set up a tent, and put foamies in it to sleep on. They had a gas stove to cook on and even folding chairs and a table.

Katie told Jeannie it made her too nervous to be in the ring with all those other horses. She said she was so glad Jeannie was Arnold's helper this year, so she could have some rest and stay out of the dust and noise of the arena. She patted her tummy. "Me and this new person are just going to take it easy this year." Jeannie was very excited at the idea that Kate was having a baby. It would be almost like having a baby brother or sister.

Jeannie loved every second of the horse show. She loved the noise, the dust, the excitement, the smell of sweaty horses and leather. They were going faster now, making circles and figure eights in the middle of the arena. The timing had to be just right to keep them all from crashing into each other. The horses snorted and pranced, lifting their long legs, with their flying feathery plumes of hair. Their tails were knotted and interlaced with ribbons to keep them from tangling with the harness. Some of the horses had their manes braided with more brightly coloured ribbons; Jeannie had spent hours that morning helping Arnold braid Sebastien and Sally's manes and tails. Her fingers still ached from all that work.

Finally, the parade was over and they left the arena to whistles, cheers and applause from the crowd. Now it was time to go back to the barns where the horses were kept, unharness, wash everything again, and have lunch. What a lot of work horses were! But they were worth it, Jeannie thought. There was nothing she would rather be doing. All those years she had lived in town, with no idea what horses were like. The idea of giving up her life with the horses when she went back to live with her mother was not something Jeannie really wanted to think about.

The first two days of the horse show flew by. The doors of Sebastien's and Sally's stalls in the barns grew decorations made of yellow, blue and red ribbons. Jeannie was busy from morning until evening. She got up at six in the morning to help feed and brush the horses. Then she had to clean their stalls, put down fresh sawdust, and carry buckets of fresh water. She ate a huge breakfast and then it was back to the barns to take the horses out, help give them a bath, braid their manes and tails, and get them ready to be hitched up to the wagon. All over the horse show grounds, other people were doing the same thing, calling greetings to each other, getting ready for another day.

Jeannie and Norma Jean spent time together every day. They had fun giving each of their horses a bath. They talked and talked about horses and about their lives. Norma Jean didn't live with her parents either. Instead, she was living with an aunt and uncle. Her mom and dad were divorced and both of them were away working. Norma Jean had pictures of her parents to show Jeannie. Her mom was working in California. Her dad was on another ranch. For some reason, neither of them could afford to look after her right now. They talked about how much they missed their moms. Norma Jean said she didn't miss her dad. He'd been mean when he was drinking, she said.

In the evening of the next to last day, they sat on the top rail of the corral fence and watched the sun go down in a haze of dust. Katie had invited Norma Jean for supper and they had all eaten hamburgers outside at a picnic table.

"I wish my mom would come home," Norma Jean said. "She's always going to come but then she has to work. She sends me pictures and stuff." She took a picture of her mom out of her pocket. Norma Jean's mom had red hair and lots of makeup.

"I can see my mom in the hospital," Jeannie said, "but there's always someone around. It's like they're worried something might happen. I wish they'd leave us alone."

"Do you like to read books, Jeannie?" Norma Jean asked.

"Yeah, my foster mom has all these old animal stories, *Black Beauty, The Black Stallion,* stuff like that.

"Hey, I read those books. They're pretty good. So, what's your foster mom like?"

"She's really nice. So is Tom." Jeannie frowned. "Sometimes they're too nice. It's like they're trying to give me everything so I'll never leave. But I have to be with my mom."

"My aunt does that too. She feels sorry for me, I can tell."
They were both quiet.

"Let's write and e-mail each other, okay, and then next year, we'll see each other again. We can meet here every year," Norma Jean said.

"Good idea," said Jeannie. "I even have my own computer in my room. My mom could never afford to get a computer."

"You're gonna miss all that stuff when you leave."

"No, I won't." Jeannie said. "It's just stuff."

"You'll miss the horses, I bet."

"Yeah, horses are so cool, especially big work horses."

"Well, I better go," Norma Jean said. "I'll see you tomorrow morning in the barn."

"Sure," said Jeannie.

But she sat on the fence a little while longer, listening to horses whinny back and forth to each other in the dusk.

The competition everyone was waiting for, the pulling competition, was the next day, Sunday afternoon. Each team of horses would have to pull a sled loaded with concrete blocks for a certain distance. The team that pulled the most weight the farthest would win. This was the first year Arnold had entered and he was very nervous about it.

He had talked to Jeannie about it late one evening while they were sitting together cleaning the shiny black harness. "The pulling contest is hard on the horses," he said. "They have to give you every bit of their strength. They have to trust their driver. They have to trust that you won't ask them to do a job that's too hard for them. If you ask them to do something and they can't do it, it breaks their big loyal hearts. They're the most amazing critters. They'll kill themselves trying to do what you want. But you can't overdo it. You can break that trust by asking them to do something too hard, especially a young team like Sebastien and Sally."

He paused then he added softly. "No young'un should have to take on too hard a job. A kid's job is to have fun, right, Jeannie the mouse? A parent's job is to keep them safe and happy. Hey, that's enough hard work and heavy thinking for one day. Off to bed with you. Morning comes awful early around here."

Sunday morning, everyone was up early. Jeannie and Norma Jean met at the barn at six o'clock, rubbing sleep out of their eyes. They had to carry hay, clean the stalls, and then take the giant horses for a bath.

The people getting their horses ready at the barns were quiet. There wasn't as much joking and calling back and forth as usual. The pulling contest was not only important; it was worth a lot of money. Ten thousand dollars was the first prize. Jeannie knew that one reason Arnold had entered the contest was to try and win the money. With the new baby coming, it would make Arnold and Katie's life a lot easier. Logging with the horses didn't make a lot of money.

The team pulling competition was the last competition

of the day. In the morning, Jeannie sat in the stands with Katie and watched the other horses go through their different classes. She knew Arnold was back at the barn, doing a lot of last minute tiny chores that didn't really need doing, trying to keep himself busy so he wouldn't be too nervous.

At last it was time for the pulling competition. All the competitors came in the ring, one at a time, the drivers walking quietly behind their teams. They lined up on the far side of the ring, beside the sled that was loaded with one layer of concrete blocks.

One by one, each team was hitched to the sled and pulled it the distance that was marked by white chalk lines. The first time, only a couple of teams were eliminated. More concrete blocks were loaded on the sled and each team took their turn pulling it again. This time several more teams were eliminated. The funniest looking team was a big black horse hitched together with a Shetland pony. But they had no difficulty pulling the sled the marked distance.

Soon the competition was down to four teams, then three. The sled was loaded again. The first team to try was the tall black horse and the Shetland pony. Their driver was an ancient looking gnome of a man, with a baseball hat on his bald head, and a ragged plaid shirt hanging out over his torn jeans.

His team was hitched to the sled. "Hiyup!" he yelled, slapping the reins on their backs. The team put their heads down and pulled, digging their powerful feet into the ground, their muscles bunching under their shining coats. Their bellies were low to the ground as they fought to drag the sled the required fifteen foot distance. But they made it.

The next team to go was a matched team of powerful Belgians. They were a beautiful golden beige colour. The feather plumes on their legs were a mix of black, white and grey hairs. Their legs were short. Their bodies looked like solid muscle. Arnold had told Jeannie and Katie that this was the best team at the fair. They held several records for the weight-pulling event. Their driver was a young man who looked quietly confident. He backed his team to the sled and watched while they were hitched. Then he inspected everything carefully. Finally, he stood behind his team, picked up the lines and said something in such a quiet voice, Jeannie couldn't hear what he said.

His team hit the end of the traces and began to pull. The dust flew from under their giant hooves as they struggled for each foot of ground. But they made it. Now it was Arnold's turn. He backed Sebastien and Sally up to the sled, took his time patting their necks as everything was hitched. Then he walked around in a big circle before he picked up the lines.

"Sal, Seb, hup, hup," he yelled, and the two giant grey horses put all their strength into tugging the sled, which now weighed 5000 pounds. Jeannie could see that the team was making a huge effort. Arnold stayed right behind them in the dust, encouraging them with his voice. Finally, they made it to the end of the track and stood still, puffing big steamy bellows of air. Jeannie was so tense she accidentally dug her fingernails into Katie's arm.

"Take it easy," Katie chuckled. "Don't pull my arm off. I might need it one of these days."

"Sorry," Jeannie gulped.

"Aw, that's okay. Here, let's hold hands. Then maybe we'll both feel better."

Another load of concrete blocks was piled on the sled. Again, the black horse and the Shetland pony went first. Despite a ferocious effort, they couldn't manage to pull the sled the required distance and were eliminated. Everyone stood up and cheered and applauded as they left the ring. The old man didn't look up, but he lifted his hat to acknowledge the cheers.

Now it was the turn of the big blond Belgians. They dug their hooves into the ground with tremendous force, heaving the sled forward in little jerks, almost falling on the ground with the tremendous effort they were making. Their driver stayed right behind them, encouraging them in a soft voice until they were past the marker and stood with their heads down, puffing madly.

Now it was Arnold's turn. Jeannie could see from the deep frown on his face that he was worried. He took his time. Finally, he picked up the lines and sent Sebastien and Sally forward. They hit the end of the traces with tremendous force but the sled barely moved. They dug down until their muscles were bunched and straining. Arnold had to keep encouraging them to go straight. Jeannie leaned forward, encouraging them with every muscle in her own body The sled moved with agonizing slowness. Finally, just short of the mark they had made before, the team stopped, their heads down, their sides heaving. Arnold went to their heads. He patted and talked to them. Then he nodded to the crew standing by, who came over and unhitched the sled.

Slowly, Arnold began to lead his team from the ring.

"This man," said the announcer, "has just done a very good thing. He's got a young team, they've done their best and he's not going to let them break their hearts trying to pull too much weight. They'll be back next year, for sure, isn't that right, Arnold?" Arnold raised his hat and grinned at the crowd, which burst into loud applause.

Jeannie jumped from her seat and dashed down the steps to the exit. "Arnold," she called. "Arnold, wait!"

He turned around and bent over so she could run into his arms. He picked her up and swung her into the air.

"Hey, there, Jeannie the queen," he laughed. "Now wasn't that just a great time. We did all right, eh?"

"But Arnold," Jeannie gasped, "you didn't win. I thought you needed the money."

"Ahh, money," he said. "Hey, we had a great time and these big babies learned a thing or two. It's not about the money, Jeannie, my beaneroo, it's about doin' right and havin' a good time. I wouldn't hurt ol' Seb and Sal for all the money in the world or ask them to do something that's beyond their strength. Remember what I said about trust, and not giving a youngster too much to handle. No amount of money would ever make up for breaking the trust in an animal's heart. Never forget that, Jeannie. That's the truth of it all and it's the only truth that matters."

He picked Jeannie up and swung her onto Sebastien's back and began to lead the team back to the barn. From all over, people called to them, "Well done, way to go, good show," the voices said. Jeannie sat up straighter on her giant grey steed. She felt as though she really were a queen. She never wanted the feeling to end.

Chapter Thirteen

The week after the Draft Horse Show, Arnold and Katie said they were so exhausted they decided to take a day off to go fishing. They asked Jeannie to check on the horses, feed the chickens and gather the eggs, and keep an eye on everything.

"Haven't been fishing in years," Arnold laughed. "Can't remember the last time I took a vacation. Maybe we'll come home with enough big trout for dinner, eh?"

Jeannie and Buddy went over to their house early the next morning. Jocko came to meet them, wagging his tail. The place felt strangely quiet. Jeannie went in the house, looked in the fridge, had a glass of lemonade and a cookie, then went back outside. She sat on the deck and tried to imagine what it would be like if this were her place. She would be able to get up every morning, look at this view, visit the horses, say to Jocko, "C'mon, mister," the way Arnold did. Everything on the place would look to her for care. She stood up, went down the steps to the road, stood there indecisively. One path led to the garden, one to the chicken coop, one to the barn. She went to the barn. The horses were grazing in the pasture. A rooster crowed from the chicken pen. The cats were curled up sleeping.

She got Billy's halter, led him in from the pasture, saddled him and headed up the mountain. It felt strange to be going off by herself, and Billy didn't like it. He tossed his head and tried to turn around, but she was a good enough rider now to make him behave.

"You be good," she said nervously. The woods were full of sunlight. Jocko and Buddy trailed at their heels. There was nothing to be afraid of.

She rode higher and higher on the mountain. Finally, she reached the pond where she and Shannon and Shirley had eaten lunch on their expedition up the mountain. The pond had a rim of dried mud around it. The leaves on the bushes were shriveled and yellow from the heat.

She slid off Billy and tied him by his halter rope so he could graze on the thin yellow grass. She wandered around the edge of the pond, looking at the deer tracks in the mud. Blue dragonflies buzzed and rattled over the still surface of the pond.

From far away, she could hear a breeze, sighing down the mountain like a giant breath. She went and sat under a yellow-leaved poplar tree. From here, she could see over the valley. She could see the river like a silver chain between two lines of trees. Farther away, mountains lay like a rumpled blue quilt with patchy clouds snagged on the treetops. The breeze lifted her hair and stroked her cheek. Buddy leaned his warm weight against her shoulder.

She sat there for a long time. Billy's eyes drooped. He stood with his head down, switching his tail against flies. A tiny brilliant red spider crawled across the rock, over her foot, and continued on its way.

"I wish I could stay here forever," she said out loud. Her voice startled the dogs, who both sat up in surprise. She knew it was time to go but she sat a little longer. Then she mounted Billy, and rode slowly down the mountain.

When she got to Arnold and Katie's, something seemed different. The horses were all gathered in a corner of the pasture, looking at something. Something was wrong. She jumped off Billy, opened the gate, remounted, and galloped across the pasture.

Something was very wrong. It was Kit Kat. Somehow, he had gotten his head and front legs through a hole in the fence. Now the wire had tightened around his belly and he wasn't able to move forward or back. Blood was running from scratches on his legs and neck. His head was down, his eyes were wild and frightened.

When he saw Jeannie, he started to struggle. The wire

tightened around his belly, and fresh blood ran down his sides.

His mother, big brown Belle, nickered anxiously. All the horses crowded forward. Jeannie ran to Kit Kat. She crouched on the ground, tried to work the wire loose, but it was hopeless. The wire was digging into his skin, through his skin. She needed to cut it. How did you cut wire?

Arnold would know but Arnold was far away. She was in charge. It was her place. The animals depended on her to look after them.

Get help. That was the first thing. She jumped back on Billy, raced him like a crazy person up the driveway to the house. Her hands were shaking but she remembered to tie him carefully to a tree before running in the house to the phone.

"Susan," she said, as soon as a voice said hello. "The baby horse is stuck in the fence. I need help."

"Oh, no, Tom's away and I don't have the car," Susan said. "Call the vet. Here's the number. But Jeannie, you'll have to cut the wire. You can't leave him there."

"How?" Jeannie said. Her voice cracked. "How do you cut wire?"

"Go the barn," Susan said, her voice sharp with fear. "Find a pair of fencing pliers. There should be some with Arnold's tools. Use the sharp part at the back to cut the wire."

Jeannie slammed the phone down, stabbed at the numbers for the vet.

"A baby horse is caught in the wire," she said. "I can't

get him free. There's no one here but me. I don't know what to do."

"Someone will come right away. Where do you live?"

"It's Arnold and Katie's place, on Blaze Creek Road."

"What's the house number?"

"I don't know."

"Okay, we'll find it, but listen, you have to get the colt out of the wire, before he suffocates. Can you find some pliers?"

"I think . . . so," Jeannie stuttered. What did pliers look like? Why didn't she know? What kind of stupid person was she, not even to know one kind of tool from another? Farmers needed to know about tools.

"Keep him standing up," the voice said. "Try to get him up to the barn. I'm on my way."

The phone clicked in her ear. Back on Billy, race to the barn. Tie him again. Run in the door. There were boxes of tools in the tack room with the saddle. Hammers, nails, a saw, those she recognized. Pliers. These things with two handles. These must be pliers. She took three different kinds, raced back to Billy, back across the pasture.

Kit Kat was sagging in the wire, breathing heavily, his eyes half closed. Billy slammed to a stop. Jeannie slid off his back and fell to her knees beside the baby.

"Hang on," she said, "just hang on."

The pliers bit into the wire but didn't cut it. Her hands weren't strong enough. She squeezed with all her might. Suddenly the wire parted. A piece of it flew back and caught her face but that didn't matter. She only had to cut two more wires and he was free.

He began to struggle again.

"Easy," she soothed. "Easy, easy."

The second wire parted with a twang. Her hands cramped. She shook them out, got the pliers on the third wire, squeezed with all her strength. There.

"C'mon, Kit Kat, c'mon." She got her arms under his belly and tried to lift him up. Belle nickered, crowded in on her. Kit Kat got his legs under himself, pushed up and stood, wobbly, but standing. The barbs on the wire had torn chunks from his skin. A flap of skin was hanging loose on his leg. Looking at it made Jeannie feel sick.

Then Jeannie felt something warm trickle down her own forehead. She put her hand up and it came away red.

"C'mon, sweet baby horse, little Kit Kat, little precious boy, come on, you can do it," hardly knowing what she was saying. She got behind him and pushed. He began to limp slowly towards the barn. Belle followed and everyone else followed behind her. The whole herd of them moved together.

Just as she got to the gate, a white truck arrived. A short brown-haired woman in a white coat jumped out, ran into the pasture.

"Okay," she said. "Let's get him in a stall. Put mom in the stall next to him. Get a halter on her and we'll lead them both in."

Jeannie ran for a halter. Her legs flew like the wind. She haltered Belle and helped get the baby in a stall. The other horses waited anxiously, looking over the pasture fence. Poor Billy was still wearing his bridle and saddle. He'd have to wait a little longer. She ran back to the vet.

"He'll be all right," said the vet. She had a strong accent. "A bit longer though, and he might have suffocated. Where is Mr. Arnold?"

"He's fishing."

"And you are here alone?"

"Yeah."

"Well, I have to sew up these tears in his skin. You will have to help me hold him. Get him in a corner of the stall. Please don't let him jump around. You must be very strong to hold him still."

Jeannie tried but Kit Kat jumped every time he saw the needle. Jeannie didn't blame him.

Finally, the vet was finished. She gave Kit Kat a shot with another huge needle and said, "He will need a shot three times a day. Tell Arnold to phone me when he gets home. You can put him in with mom now."

Then she patted the baby, climbed in her truck and drove away. Jeannie was left alone with the silence. She put Kit Kat in with Belle, went outside, took the saddle and bridle off Billy, put them away, gave him some treats and let him go, then sat on the bench by the barn door. She put her head down. Blackness swirled behind her eyes.

If this was what owning a farm meant, maybe she wasn't ready for it just yet. Her hands and legs were shaking.

Slowly she walked up to the house to phone Susan.

"Tom will be home in a few minutes," Susan said. "We're coming right over. Jeannie, please, just take it easy until we get there."

Jeannie sank into a chair. When Tom and Susan finally arrived, it felt so good to feel their arms around her, feel Susan's hands smoothing her hair, fussing over her cut forehead. She fell asleep in the car on the way home, her hand clasped in Susan's hand. Tom had stayed behind to keep an eye on things and wait for Arnold and Katie to come home.

Chapter Fourteen

Arnold and Katie came over the next morning full of praise for Jeannie's quick thinking. Kit Kat healed well. Jeannie visited him every day to check on him and hold him still while Arnold gave him a shot of penicillin.

Then school started and Jeannie had all the excitement of buying new school clothes and supplies. Every day, when she got off the big yellow bus after school, Buddy was waiting at the bus stop and Susan was waiting in the kitchen with cookies or popcorn. These days, the world was a blaze of colour, orange and red maple trees beside the gate to the yard, tamarack trees beacons of bright gold on the hills above the road.

Today, Jeannie had been singing out loud as she came up the drive, Buddy leaping and jumping beside her. She couldn't believe how beautiful everything was. The kittens were playing outside on the lawn, rolling over and over in the rustling leaves.

Just after she came in, the phone rang. "It's your mother," Susan said. Her face looked strange. She held out the phone to Jeannie.

Jeannie grabbed the phone.

"Jeannie," said a familiar voice in her ear. "Jeannie, they're going to let me out. I can go home. I can get my own place. You can be with me again. Oh, Jeannie, I've missed you so much. We can finally be a family again. Oh, at last. I've waited so long for this moment."

Jeannie sank into a chair at the table. "Umm, that's great, Mom," she managed to say. Her thoughts were in a whirl. She couldn't leave right now, she thought. Just this afternoon, they had had tryouts for the school play. They were going to do a musical play called "Six Dancing Princesses," and Jeannie's teacher, Mrs. Palmer, had said she thought Jeannie would be great for one of the lead parts.

"Jeannie, are you okay? Are you sure this is what you want? I know you really like those people, but Jeannie, I'm your mother. I need you to be with me. Everything is going to be better now. I know things used to be kind of mixed up, but I feel a lot better. I'm strong now. I can manage. I know I'll do even better with you to help me. And Jeannie, it looks like I might be able to go back to school. I'm so excited."

"When are you getting out?" Jeannie blurted. What a

dumb way to put it, she thought. Like her mom was being let out of jail.

"Right away," her mom said. "They told me this morning but I waited to phone you until after school. Oh, I'm so happy. I'll have to look for a place for us, a nice little apartment, somewhere we can be close to the mall."

An apartment. Oh, no. Jeannie began to feel as if the walls of the kitchen were shrinking, closing in on her. The mall. Her mom loved going there. Jeannie hated going to the mall. Why did she feel this way? She should be so happy. This is what she had wanted. This is what she had waited for, for so long. She and her mother would be together at last. They would be a family again.

"Jeannie, are you still there?" said her mom's voice. "You're so quiet."

"I'm fine, Mom," Jeannie said. "I mean, I'm really, really happy. This is great. I can hardly wait to see you again." That much, at least, was true.

"Okay, Jeannie, gotta go," her mom said. "I'll phone you as soon as I get a place. Then I can let my social worker know and she'll come and get you. We'll be together again soon. Bye, my sweetie."

Jeannie hung up the phone. Susan put a glass of milk and a plate of cookies on the table in front of her.

"My mom's getting out," Jeannie said. She didn't want to hurt Susan's feelings but she had to tell her. Susan was looking at her with questions written all over her face. "She wants me to come live with her again. She's feeling a lot better. She says we can be a family again."

"That's great, Jeannie," Susan said. She sounded absolutely miserable. "I'm going to make us a very special dinner, to celebrate. Maybe I'll make a chocolate cake. Would you like that?"

"Sure, thanks," Jeannie heard her voice squeak. Susan opened a cupboard door and got out a cookbook. Jeannie drank her milk and ate her cookies. There was a bowl of crisp apples on the table. She picked out a big red one. Then she carried her new backpack up to her room. She took her homework out of the backpack and put it on her desk, next to the new computer Susan and Tom had bought her when school started. She got a pen out of her pack and started to do her homework. But she stopped, and sat staring at the wall. What was the point? Soon she'd be in a new school, a big school, trying to make new friends and fit in. No one would care if she'd done her homework at this school or not. Maybe she'd quit going to school.

No one would be there to defend her if the other kids teased her about having a mom who was crazy, a mom who'd been in the psych ward. She'd be on her own. She wouldn't even have Buddy. He'd have to stay behind with Susan and Tom. She'd be on her own.

Why, why, why, had any of this happened, her mom getting sick and now, just as unexpectedly, getting better? It was all so unfair. Jeannie had been getting by before, with just her mom. Things weren't great. But she hadn't known any better. She hadn't known about horses, and pet kittens, and friends and riding her bike down a country road through piles of yellow leaves. When she left here, she would miss everybody and everything so much. She felt like she had two families now. That wasn't something she had ever planned on. She didn't want to have to choose. It was exactly what Arnold had been talking about at the horse show. It was too hard. She shouldn't have to choose. She should be able to have all the people she loved be a part of her life. This was too heavy a burden for her. It was too confusing. Parts of it were happy. Parts of it were horribly sad. She couldn't tell how she was supposed to feel.

Good smells floated up from the kitchen, the smell of chocolate cake baking, the smell of roast beef cooking. Jeannie's stomach rumbled. How could she be so hungry and so miserable at the same time? Susan seemed to think most of life's problems could be fixed by lots of good food. She was always cooking, baking, cleaning. When she wasn't doing that, she was sewing, or gardening.

Jeannie tried to remember what her mother's cooking was like. Her mother liked to eat out. She liked to go to the food court at the mall. She liked cheesey mushroom soup from a can and toast. She drank a lot of coffee. Jeannie used to like to drink pretend coffee with her mom. She put lots of milk and sugar in hot water to make it taste better.

The last apartment they had stayed at together had been

on the second floor of a building that was all stores in front. One of them was a Chinese restaurant, one of them a video store. Jeannie remembered when they lived there that the smell of Chinese food cooking always made her feel hungry. They had to go up to the apartment on the stairs that led past the garbage bins. It always stank back there.

After a while, Susan called Jeannie and Tom for supper. Although supper was supposed to be some kind of celebration, everyone was very quiet. After supper, Jeannie got up without being told and piled the supper dishes next to the sink. She put the dishes in the dishwasher and the sink and then rinsed all the pots. Susan always did those later. Then she got the box of cat food and went outside, down to the pottery shed to feed the kittens. They came running when they saw her, rubbing against her legs. They were almost full-grown now. Tom and Susan were going to keep Jeannie's kitten and give the rest away.

Buddy came and jumped around her, wanting to play. He went and got the soccer ball and laid it in front of her. "C'mon," his eyes said. But Jeannie had no heart for playing. It was already getting dark. The wind coming down off the mountains was cold. Jeannie went back in the house.

"I'm going over to Arnold's," she said.

"But Jeannie, it's already dark."

"I'll use the light on my bike."

"But it's late. You have to do homework."

"It's okay," said Tom quietly. "We understand. Phone us

when you're ready to come home and we'll come get you."

Jeannie got her bike out of the shed and headed down the road. Buddy ran behind her. The wind whistled through her jacket. The road seemed long and lonesome. In the summer, in the bright sun, it seemed to take only a few minutes. Now at night, in the dark, the road seemed to stretch on forever.

But when she got to Arnold and Katie's house, they weren't home. The lights were on in the horse barn. The horses were glad to see her and greeted her with nickers and friendly nudges. She went from stall to stall, giving each animal a pat, a scratch, and a handful of horse crunchies. She got a brush and spent some time cleaning them up. They nudged her with their soft noses, then went back to munching hay. They seemed so at home, in their cozy barn. A radio was quietly playing country music. Jeannie wondered what to do next. She sat on a prickly pile of hay bales at the door, watching for lights in the driveway. She curled her arms around her knees. The wind was getting colder. Everyone else had a place they belonged, she thought. Everyone here was so settled, so sure of where they wanted to be. But Jeannie didn't belong anywhere.

Once she had been so sure that her place was with her mother. Their bond was strong and unbreakable. But then against her will it had been stretched and torn and Jeannie's life had changed. Who would look after the animals when she was gone? Would a new foster child come to live in her beautiful room? How would Buddy ever understand why she wasn't there. Who would he play with now?

Shannon and Shirley would always have lots of friends. They would continue to live on Blaze Creek Road and they'd go riding without her. She'd never teach Caitlin to ride, as she had promised.

But she knew she loved her mother. She missed her. She needed to be with her.

She put her head down on her knees and closed her eyes. She would go live with her mother, but she would never forget the horses and maybe, someday, when she was older, she could come back. She had to come back. She had found something wonderful that she had never dreamed existed. Now she was going to lose it. She wanted to cry but she was too miserable. She felt like a frozen chunk of misery, sitting in the dark cold barn.

She must have fallen asleep because the next thing she knew, she heard a gentle voice in her ear.

"Hey, Jeannie the mouse queen McBean, how are things?"

Arnold sat down beside her on the hay bales. "Hope you gave all my babies a treat," he added.

"Yeah," she said miserably. "I had to refill Sebastien's water bucket. And Kit Kat had burrs in his tail. I cleaned them out. It took a long time."

"Good for you," Arnold said. "I don't know how I'm going to manage without your help, Ms. McBean."

Jeannie felt the tears start in her eyes again. She put her

head back down on her knees. She hated crying in front of people.

Arnold was quiet for a long time. Then he said softly, "You know, I have an idea that your mom is really going to need your help. It's not going to be easy getting her life back together again, after what she's been through. Sometimes people can be pretty mean to someone who has an illness like your mom. But you're the kind of person a person can rely on. You're like Sebastien there, strong and solid. When something needs doing, you get on and do it. If someone's lost, you go find them. Your mom loves you very much, but she's also very lucky to have you to depend on."

"It's not fair," Jeannie said bitterly. "It's like what you said, like the pulling contest. I shouldn't have to do this. I shouldn't have to choose. It's too hard."

"Yeah, you're right there," Arnold said. "But there's one little difference. Sebastien and Sally were there because I made them be. They pulled that weight because it's what they know how to do and because their big faithful hearts tell them to do their best no matter what. But this here situation you've got to deal with isn't anyone's fault. It's just one of them situations that falls in a person's lap some-times, and then all you can do is give it your best with all you got in you. And that's a lot, Jeannie McBean. You're bright and good and you've got a great heart. You've made everybody here care about you."

They were both silent again. Jeannie was thinking hard

about what Arnold had said. She remembered when she thought he was the weirdest person she had ever met. Now she was going to miss him most of all. The tears were running faster now.

"Hey now," Arnold said, "What are all those tears for? You can be with your mom again. That's what you want most, right?"

"Yeah, I guess so," Jeannie choked out.

"But you're going to miss your new life here, is that it?" Jeannie couldn't talk. She nodded. Then she hid her face in her sleeve and sobbed.

Arnold put his big strong arm around her shoulders.

"Jeannie," he said, "listen up, I've got something important to tell you and I want you to listen carefully to my words."

Then he added in his soft voice, "I know you'll miss us, and we'll miss you right back, because that's what people who love each other do. But you can come visit any time. You can come summers, weekends, holidays. Buddy will miss you but he'll wait for you to come back. We all will. We'll bring your mom here one day for a visit, show her horses don't bite. Would you like that?"

He waited. Jeannie took her face out of her sleeve and stared at him. A tiny warm flame started in the middle of the cold chunk of ice inside her.

"Jeannie, we're your other family now. We'll always be here. We won't let go if you don't. The horses need you. Me and Katie need you to be a pal to that new little person that's coming along. Tom and Susan need you a lot. You've made a big difference in their lives. Your friends need you. You'll go away for a while and we'll all miss you like crazy and then you'll come back. That's what relatives do. All their lives. But they're still family, no matter what."

Jeannie took a deep breath. Family. Her family. Could it really be true? What if they forgot about her?

"But I'm not really part of your family," she choked out, "I don't really belong here."

"Well now," Arnold drawled. "I've always figured there's two kinds of families in this world, the family you're born to, and the people you choose as family, kind of like your own heart's family. No reason why you can't have both. My neighbours here, this community, this valley, they're like a family I've chosen. We look after each other. And you're a part of that now. A part of all of us. Don't let go of us, Jeannie. That's all you have to do. Just let us into your heart the way you've come into ours. You can come here any time. We'll always be your family. Always. I promise. And you know I keep my promises."

Jeannie was silent, thinking hard. She remembered when she first met Arnold. She had been so scared, and so angry. She hadn't wanted to trust him at all. Now she knew he was kind and honest and totally dependable. If he told her something, she could believe it. So it must be true. She had two families now. She didn't have to choose.

"Okay," she said. She took a deep breath. Her heart felt suddenly light as a feather, as if her blood was doing a little dance of joy all through her veins. The tiny flame inside her grew bigger and warmed her all over. "I'll do my best. I won't let go. But please, please, don't forget about me."

"Jeannie, I swear you're getting to be just like your other mom. She sure does worry about every little thing," said Arnold. "I'd better run you home, you know. Susan's been phoning every five minutes. That woman cares a lot about you. They're going to miss you something terrible, you know, both she and Tom."

"She sure does worry," said Jeannie. "I guess that's what mothers do."

"Guess so," said Arnold. "And dads too. Guess I'm going to find out all about that." Jeannie remembered Katie telling her that she and Arnold's baby would be born next spring. Arnold had been so excited when he found out that he was going to be a dad that he had jumped in the air and whooped out loud.

"How soon do you think I can take the baby riding?" asked Jeannie.

"Dunno," said Arnold. "I don't know that much about babies. Guess I'll have to learn a lot, real fast. But I'll tell you what. We'll bring him or her down to the barn right away, let the horses say hello so they know all about this new person arriving."

"Good idea," said Jeannie. "That's a really good idea." She

leaned against Arnold and he put his arm around her. Then he stood up and smiled. Arnold reached down and took her hand and swinging their arms together, they walked together out of the lighted barn and up the long driveway to the house.

A NOTE ABOUT HORSE LOGGING

Horse logging is still carried on in many parts of Canada. Horses can often work in places that are too steep or rough for machines; they are also used in areas where loggers want to avoid hurting the environment.

The horses used in horse logging are called draft horses, heavy horses or work horses. Some of the breeds of draft horses are Percherons, Clydesdales, or Belgians.

Draft horses are very gentle, even though they are so huge. They are also intelligent: they learn to start, stop, back up, go right or left — just from the driver's commands.

Draft horses were very important in Canadian history. They were used in logging, in farming, in clearing land, in pulling wagons and in carrying heavy loads of all kinds.

ABOUT THE AUTHOR

Luanne Armstrong lived on an organic farm in the Kootenay region of B.C. for many years, where she learned about draft horses and horse logging as a young girl. She completed a BFA in Creative Writing at the University of Victoria and then worked at a variety of jobs, including coordinating women's groups, teaching at a First Nations College, and working in Indonesia with an environmental organization. She has taught Creative Writing at the University of Alberta, the College of the Rockies and the Kootenay School of Arts in Nelson. In 1999, she moved to Vancouver. She has an MFA in Creative Writing from the University of B.C. in Vancouver. She was the Berton House writer in residence in Dawson City, Yukon from September to December 2000. She has written three previous books for children, two adult books and two books of poetry. She is also the managing editor of Hodgepog Books, which publishes early chapter books for children.